THE ARECA NUT TREE AND OTHER STORIES

THE ARECA NUT TREE AND OTHER STORIES

Contemporary Women's Writing from Assam

Selected and Translated by

Ranjita Biswas

Vitasta

Published by
Renu Kaul Verma
Vitasta Publishing Pvt Ltd
2/15, Ansari Road, Daryaganj
New Delhi - 110 002
info@vitastapublishing.com

ISBN: 978-93-90961-68-9

First Edition 2022
MRP ₹450

Edited by Shailaja Nair
Typeset & Cover Design by Somesh Kumar Mishra
Printed by Chaman Enterprises, New Delhi

Foreword

As per extant records, Aai Padmapriya, a poetess belonging to the 16th century was the first woman to make her foray into the annals of Assamese literature. She was followed by Padmavati Debi Phukanani, a prose fiction writer, almost three centuries later in 1844. The contributions of these two stalwarts are important to note in order to understand the place of women writers in Assamese literature. Compared with a major part of the country, the position of women in Assamese society is more elevated due to the influence of the liberal tribal society and its close association with Assamese culture, and also, the assimilation of western education and culture over time. Both these factors have boosted the social, cultural and intellectual consciousness of women writers in Assam.

In the post-Independence period, women writers played an outstanding role by contributing to *Ramdhenu*, a premier literary publication of the day. Among the trailblazers in the sphere of modern Assamese literature are Sneha Debi and Nirupama Borgohain (both Sahitya Akademi awardees), and Indira Goswami (a Jnanpith winner), all of whom engaged in scrutinising women's perspectives in their writing. The legacy has been carried on by eminent writers such as Arupa Patangia Kalita and Manorama Das Medhiand others.

This anthology, selected and translated by Ranjita Biswas, comprises stories from 14 Assamese women writers from the last decade of the 20th century. Their writings reflect issues that concern women and which have more or less remained unexplored. Two factors created a profound impact on the socio-cultural aspect of the Assamese community, stoking new trends in Assamese literature in recent times. First, the liberalisation of the economy at the beginning of the 1990s and the social unrest following globalisation, and second, the failure of regionalism that led to the rise of a brand of ultra-regionalism and armed rebellion, both guided by the ideological principle of projecting the Assamese people as a community that has been perpetually neglected, and forever at the receiving end of the powers that be. Against this background of political and economic changes, women have had to face even more challenges.

The short fiction of contemporary Assamese women often reflect these complexities through sincere and true-to-life portraits. However, these writers are not confined to women-centric subjects alone. Taking into consideration a broader humanitarian perspective, they have written stories that have broken the boundary of being simply women's stories and gone beyond to become representations of great human experiences of conflict, confusion and hope.

It can be said with confidence that with her beautiful translation and qualitative selection of stories, Biswas gives the pan-Indian reader an insight into modern Assamese literature, particularly short fiction, which arguably is one of the best in this genre in the sphere of Indian regional literature today.

A look at the writers featured here is perhaps in order.

Bonti Senchowa has brought symbolic illustrations into her stories almost like in poetry, but her tales always talk about the harsh realities of life. Humanity and sensitivity are powerful tools in her stories to express social consciousness and protest against exploitation. The story *Mini* depicts a character who at last finds the courage to resist.

Leena Sarma focuses on issues of modern life and queries about existential conflict through her prose writings and stories. Her works often travel to areas where the essence of our existence is scrutinised.

Maini Mahanta has written several stories on the complexity of man-woman relationships. In our modern existence, people may live with an illusion of happiness in a relationship but the very fact that they carry on in loneliness often forms the centre of Mahanta's stories.

In most of the stories of **Monikuntala Bhattacharjya**, the characters belong to small towns but their lives prove to be no less complicated than in the cities. Expressions of loneliness and generosity of love along with insights into the woman's inner world are depicted in her stories with great understanding.

Kavyashree Mahanta creates her stories like a psychological overview rather than a simple narrative of day-to-day experiences. Hence, her characters are not merely created to express emotions; behind them remains always a stream of conscious effort.

In contemporary Assamese literature, **Moushumi Kandali** has a notable status. Using musical imagery and expressions, her stories are good examples of art and intellectual expression melding together. At the same time, her stories have a strong socio-cultural discourse running through them that offer the possibility of drawing multiple interpretations. Her stories try to reassess the essence of humanity through philosophical query. Her language and delineations often create a cinematic effect.

The problems of rural life, the confusion and conflict created by a poverty-stricken economy, the simplicity and cultural significance that still exist amidst the poor, are some of the issues successfully depicted in the stories of **Anamika Borah**. The depth of the subject matter and the use of language are most striking in her stories.

Ratna Bharali Talukdar's stories cover numerous contemporary socio-historical issues. From terrorism to ethnic clashes, globalisation to political restlessness and its impact on the common people, and the condition of people caught in such circumstances, are expressed beautifully in her stories. Her powerful representations of the harsh realities of life often lead the reader to examine those realities again.

With the strong articulation of language and a poetic narrative, **Gitali Borah's** stories explore the mystery behind human relationships. She throws light on the multifaceted lives of people living in big cities with great skill.

Monica Devee takes tradition, folktales-based composite text of rural lives, and cultural identity as the source for her stories. Many of them reflect cross-cultural conflicts.

Among the other four writers, **Juri Borah Borgohain's** social reality, **Ruplekha Devi's** expressions of dream-like experiences, **Gayatri Doley's** folk life-based experimentations –all create individual identities. In the stories of the youngest writer **Juri Barua**, portrayal of the artistic perspective of the individual and social issues express a strong criticism of an exploitative culture.

This new generation of women writers articulate a variety of experiences culled from the inner world of women against the backdrop of modern life. However, their works go beyond the individual to achieve a broader humanistic significance.

Through these evocative stories Ranjita Biswas attempts to introduce readers from outside Assam to the range of Assamese women's writing set in contemporary times. It will surely add value to the growing interest in regional literature in India and abroad.

—Arindam Borkakati

Educatonist, critic, essayist and editor

About The Authors

Anamika Borah is well-known as a forceful contemporary writer. With a keen observation of people and society, her stories often focus on subaltern sensibilities within mainstream Assamese society. Borah has published four short-story collections, three novels and one children's book. She teaches in a school in Dhing in central Assam.

Bonti Senchowa has marked her space in Assamese literature by engaging the readers in intricate plot constructions and suggestiveness. Critics have praised her subtle use of language and symbolism while telling stories of people caught between tradition and the angst of modern times. She has published four collections of short stories and one novel.

Gayatri Doley is known for her portrayal of society with an unblinking eye. The Mising tribe, to which she belongs, appears in many of her stories. She regularly contributes to popular Assamese magazines and reads out her short stories at different forums, including the Sahitya Akademi sessions.

Geetali Borah, journalist and editor, is currently Associate Editor, *Prakash*, a monthly literary magazine published by the Publication Board, Assam. The feminine perspective is noticeable in her stories. She has published six short-story collections and two novels. She has received several prestigious literary awards, including a special award from the Asom Sahitya Sabha for her first novel *Nirobodhi Noiranjona Buddhajaya* based on the life of Buddha's wife Yashodhara.

Juri Baruah is one of the most talented writers on the Assamese literary scene today. Her stories often echo her political sensibility and the characters tend to belong to the periphery of the society. Baruah's stories appear regularly in well-known Assamese magazines. Her short-story collection *Bebilonar Din Bebilonar Rati* was published in 2016. Baruah teaches in a college in Jorhat, Assam.

Juri Borah Borgohain, author, environmentalist and social activist, is the first woman journalist from Majuli, the largest inhabited river island in the world. After working for seven years as a journalist, she taught in various colleges before taking up full-time writing. She has written eight novels, 23 novellas and is a regular contributor to newspapers and magazines.

Kavyashree Mahanta started writing for leading Assamese periodicals in the early 1990s. Primarily known as a fiction writer, she also dabbles in various literary genres like poetry, non-fiction, travelogues and translations. She has published four collections of short stories, four novels and three translations including Emily Bronte's *Wuthering Heights*. Professionally, she belongs to the Assam Civil Service.

Leena Sarma, novelist and short-story writer, has to her credit nine novels, including one in English, and two short-story collections. Her novels deal with social and historical themes while her short stories delve into the complex human psyche by examining people from a different perspective. Earlier, she worked as an officer with the Indian Railway Service. Currently, she is posted as Member/Technical, Railway Claims Tribunal, Guwahati.

Maini Mahanta is editor of a women's magazine and a well-known TV personality. She has been writing fiction since the 1990s. Known for a pronounced feminist tone, readers discern in her work an empathy for the deprived section of people living on the fringes of urban life. She has published 10 collections of short stories and two novels.

Manika Devee blends local flavour in the language of her stories to great effect. Portrayal of the rural life is her forte. She has received several prestigious literary awards for her fiction. She has published eight books of short stories. She debuted as a lyricist in 2017 at Akashvaani, Guwahati. She works in a school in Guwahati.

Monikuntala Bhattacharjya is one of the most versatile Assamese writers today. Till date, she has published 20 novels, six short-story collections, four collections of poetry, three novels for children, and numerous translations. Bhattacharjya has received more than 18 literary awards for her fiction. *Ishu*, a Rajat Kamal award-winning film, is based on her story on witch hunting.

Moushumi Kandali is a bilingual creative writer, art historian and translator. She has published nine books so far and has received several literary awards. She was part of the Indian writers' entourage to the Frankfurt Book Fair in 2006. Her stories have been translated into various Indian languages as well as German and English. Kandali taught literary and visual arts at Ambedkar University, Delhi, for several years. Currently, she teaches at the Department of Cultural Studies at Tezpur Central University.

Ratna Bharali Talukdar, journalist and author, is a recipient of the Ram Nath Goenka Award and the Laadli Media National Award for journalism. She has also won several awards for her fiction. Talukdar has published three collections of short stories and one novel. She is the executive editor of nezine.com, a bilingual e-magazine in English and Assamese.

Ruplekha Devi was brought up in the Nilachal hills, mythical abode of Goddess Kamakhya. In many of her works, the ambience of the area is palpable. She often writes in the unique dialect of the Assamese language spoken there; a hybrid of the many languages brought in by pilgrims over centuries. A performing artiste, she had to change track due to a serious health issue and now concentrates on writing and teaching. She has received several awards for her novels and short stories.

Contents

The Areca Nut Tree

Manika Devee

The man was eager. He made overtures to his wife. It was tacit. A man does not waste time with words. The wife should instinctively understand that her husband wants to have sex with her. And this bed where they retired for the night was meant for it, wasn't it? There was no excuse for not understanding this simple truth. The man was not ready to wait. His body burnt with desire.

He tossed and turned restlessly a couple of times. The wooden bed shook. How could any woman not respond to this invitation? Yet she lay like a piece of wood beside him.

Original Title: Kakini

Yes, like a piece of wood. She lay there as though she was dead. The pain was unbearable. She was unable to lie down on her back and so turned to one side of her body to get some relief. Her back bore witness to the severe beating she had received from her husband that day. The streaks of coagulated blood criss-crossed her back. The stick he used to restrain the cows almost broke in two when he beat her with it. She shivered at the memory. And after all this, what did he expect? That she would dance around him like a butterfly? She ground her teeth, livid with anger.

The man was also gnashing his teeth in anger. The rage that overcame him at midday spurted out again. Well, at that time she had taken too long to pour water into the glass from the pitcher, but now? Now there was no reason to be late in responding to him. Her body was full of promise, the lush figure was there to be taken. All he wanted was a little response from her. But she did not show any interest. Oh, how could one bear this show of defiance? What was he going to do? Beat her up again? Every strike would give some relief to his increasing impatience to devour her body. No, it was not possible now. His desire could not be tamed in any other way. He was not going to wait for her to come to him willingly. He was going to enjoy his right as a husband. He snatched away the *aanchal* covering her breasts.

You can take away a piece of cloth covering the

breasts easily, but can you whittle down the mountain of bitterness building inside her heart? She jumped down from the bed, opened the bamboo door and walked out onto the veranda without fear. Whom would she fear anyway? The granary at the corner, with legs like bamboo poles? The kitchen, looming like a monster, that exhaled fumes all day? Or the big room, on the opposite side, like a witch's lair where her mother-in-law and her two sisters-in-law slept? The house, full of sounds during the day, was now silent, each corner confined to its own lair as if wrapped under a comfortable quilt.

The courtyard was awash in silvery moonlight. But, perhaps because of her tears streaming down her cheeks like rain, she saw only a cloudy sky.

She was the only daughter in her family. Her *pita* (father) never called her anything but *Ai* (my little mother). Her older brother would wait to eat even a morsel of food till his *bhoni* (beloved sister) joined him. If her mother scolded her for any reason, they would rise to her defence. And this man, her husband, never once asked her, 'Did I hurt you too much? I don't know how it happened in my rage. Come, let me look at your back, take off your blouse.' But why should he look at her back? What was there to see anyway? God had given that portion of the body to women to receive beatings from men. Right! It was quite a neglected part of her body.

And what grave mistake had she committed to deserve

such punishment, to have her back covered with bruises? Admitted, he had returned from the field tired after a long day. He had asked for a glass of water. Through an opening in the reed wall of the kitchen, she had got a glimpse of his sunburnt face. But she was busy at that time. The wok was on the firewood stove and the oil in it was smoking as she prepared to season the *dal* (lentil curry). Though the house was full of people, there was no one around whom she could ask to watch over the wok. They were, however, all too ready to criticise her when they sat down to lunch. Too much salt, the curry had a burnt smell, the gourd was under-cooked, etc., etc. Like the various bowls arranged around their brass plates at lunchtime, their complaints were numerous and assorted.

She took off the hot pan from the wooden fire. Just when she poured the glass of water, he came at her. He caught hold of her thick hair and shouted, 'Can't you hear me? Should I wait the whole day for a glass of water? I have spent all day under the sun and here she is traipsing around like a peacock. *Saali, haramzadi* (obscenities)!'

Her long hair had loosened from the bun. But even the thick hair could not save her back.

His shouts broke the silence of the night, 'Showing off your temper, are you? I'll cut you in two, you'll see!'

Leaning against the bamboo pole supporting the veranda, she wept silently, like the first wife spurned by the king.

Other members in the house who were half-asleep woke up with a start. They tried to listen intently from their beds. Why was the son creating a ruckus at this time of the night? Oh, good, good! There was nothing to worry about. There was no regret that their sleep had been disturbed. The daughter-in-law had failed to bring him under her thumb after all. The man remained a man, as it should be. The new bride could not change him, even the nuptial bed could not weaken his manliness. He was strong, he was his own man, as he had demonstrated in the afternoon today. He would remain so; he was not going to neglect his mother and sisters at the behest of this new woman in the house. Ah, what a relief! They went back to their dream-laden sleep, unworried and relieved.

The man's loud voice resounded in the room. The midnight slumber stirred uncertainly. But his manhood had not weakened; it stood proudly like a fort, as it had since time immemorial, unchallenged in its declaration of power. Inside the fort, fighters became restless; they declared war. They must secrete themselves in a secret place and declare victory for the fort. What would he do now? He was the owner of the fort. Without establishing his right, he could not rest. He felt a little helpless as well.

He came out of the room. Moonlight flooded the world outside. She was standing there, holding onto the bamboo pole. A soft breeze rippled through her carelessly wrapped *sador* to cover her upper body. Her back was bare. She had taken off her blouse before retiring to bed. The man stood behind her and grabbed her. Both jumped in shock.

What was this he was touching? Even his palms, coarse with hard labour, could feel the unevenness of her back – like a smooth, earthen floor wrecked by a *kumoti* insect ruthlessly trying to dig its way out. Hot steam seemed to evaporate from her wounded body. He felt himself burning in that heat. Ah! The pain! She croaked with agony at his touch. She did not utter a word but he wanted to say so many things. 'What have I done to you, my *koina,* my bride, why did I do this? I didn't realise...' But not a word came out of his mouth. They caught in his throat and the half-said words seemed to be full of unshed tears.

He wanted to destroy the foundation of the house; he wanted to break down the earthen wall with his spade; he looked at his hands and wanted to crush them on a stone; he wanted to hit his head against the wall. What had happened to him at that moment in the afternoon? What had driven him to beat her up like this? He remembered now, yes, he remembered. He had beaten her mercilessly with the stick he used on the cows.

The rush of blood that drove him to her now lost its steam. There was a strange pain in his body, familiar to him all these years. She turned to look at him. The body of the man, hardened with labour, was ramrod straight.

It was a physique she knew well. But had she met this stranger before? He seemed to lean towards her as though he wanted to take shelter in her body, and rest his head on her breast. He seemed more wounded than her. She turned to the familiar body and held the stranger's hands tenderly. At that very moment, he turned his back to the people in the main room with their happy dreams and held his wife close to his chest.

Coming back into the room, he lighted the lamp. She was lying on the bed with her back exposed. The pain was returning. But if he came nearer it would disappear, she knew. Yes, he came and sat next to her. He brought the lamp to examine the lacerated skin on her back. The swollen ribbons of flesh shone in the light. The other parts were in shadow.

He blew out the lamp. There was no more need for light. His heart was now illuminated. Like her injured back, his heart was in pain too. The burning sensation in his chest and in her back merged. Both the wounded joined together in body and soul.

In the morning as soon as he got up, he got busy fashioning out long strips from a bamboo plant. He had to secure the fence around the patch of land behind the house. He had recently planted a few rows of Kakini, a variety of the Areca nut tree. It was almost finished, only a few more were left, and he would be done. Unless he made the fence stronger, the cows and goats would feed on the plants. He decided he would continue with the task till he got his bowl of tea.

His sisters emerged from their room rubbing their eyes still looking half-asleep. They sat on the trunk of a log lying next to him. They seemed even frailer than the strips he was making from the slim Bijuli bamboo tree. Their mouths opened wide as they yawned.

One of the two asked, almost shouting, '*Bou*! Couldn't you give a few grains to the pigeons? See how they are creating a ruckus!'

'No, no, they are fighting with each other for the grains. Go to the front of the granary, you will see how they are crowding over the food,' she called out from the kitchen.

But how could they go there now? The arrival of the pigeons had coincided with the courtyard being bathed in sunlight. Surely, their half-asleep eyes couldn't bear the strong rays!

The sisters got up slowly and cleaned their teeth with sticks of the Bhot-era tree and spat out in a corner of the courtyard that had been freshly swept by their brother's wife a while earlier.

The knife was a little blunt and he found it difficult to shape the bamboo strips to his satisfaction. He liked them smooth and shining. Should he sharpen the knife on the stone near the granary, he wondered. As he was about to get up, his wife brought him tea and snacks.

He took the brass bowl of tea from her. Until he could sip the tea, he felt rather irritable. He shelved his plan to sharpen the knife. Better to have the tea first, he decided.

He looked at his wife as she turned to go back inside. She had changed her soiled night clothes. She had already had her bath and put on a new set of the two-piece *mekhela-sador* dress. He could smell the soap that clung to her freshly washed clothes. She walked fast over the zigzag impressions on the earthen courtyard made by the broom when she was sweeping it. As she entered the kitchen again she addressed her sisters-in-law, 'Your tea is ready. Please come and have it.'

'You've poured the tea already? We haven't even finished cleaning our teeth. Ah, now the tea will get cold. We can't have cold tea, surely,' they objected.

If her two sisters-in-law expressed disagreement, nobody could change it. She dithered not knowing what to do. Should she heat the tea again? Would it become bitter if she did so? Or should she make a fresh cup of tea? She had seen them brushing their teeth, that's why she had made the tea. She felt a little helpless. All the while she tried her best but somehow could not keep up with their demands. With a sinking feeling, she stood uncertainly on the doorstep of the kitchen.

It was like a drowning man clutching a straw when she heard her husband's strong voice. No, it was not a piece of straw. He had come in a boat to rescue her.

'They will take their tea at their pleasure. You come with me. Come, let's finish planting the areca nut trees today. I'll dig the holes and you will put the saplings in.'

She wanted to jump into the boat, but she hesitated. What was he saying? She should go to plant the saplings now? But who would finish all the chores in the kitchen? Her mother-in-law was yet to get up from the bed. As soon as she did, she would expect hot water to be kept ready for her. She would also have to start preparations for lunch. The younger sister-in-law had just secured admission in a college. She had to be served lunch on time so that she was not late for college, otherwise there would be trouble. She herself had never had the chance to even cross the threshold of a college. She was in Class 9 when her marriage happened. How could she comprehend the demands of a college education?

She looked at her husband. Was he making fun of her? Or, had some strange madness taken hold of him? He commanded, 'Go, finish your tea. I'll wait for you.'

At last, his sisters woke up to the fact that something had changed. Their brother was not making a fool of their *bou* (sister-in-law) after all. He really meant it. What kind of conspiracy was this? How could a man change so much overnight? They looked at their sister-in-law in anger. She must have fed him with some magic potion, otherwise how could he be so attentive to her suddenly?

She could feel their eyes boring into her like sharp

needles. She could guess why they were angry with her. But her man was also waiting. If she kept him waiting any longer, he would get angry. She stood uncertainly. She tried to protest feebly, 'When Ai gets up, I have to give her hot water.'

'Oh, isn't there anyone else in this house to do that? Listen to what I am saying,' his voice was already sounding irritated.

He dashed into the kitchen, brushing past her, and brought the glass of tea and pushed it towards her, 'Now drink it fast and come with me! Don't argue unnecessarily. My sisters can manage the kitchen chores for the time being.'

With one hand he held his wife's wrist and with the other the bamboo strips. He would repair the fence first and then would start the planting the saplings – together with his wife.

His mother had now woken up too. She could not afford to keep lying under the quilt anymore. Danger was looming ahead. What she was afraid all along was now perhaps happening. She blocked their path and demanded, 'Why are you shouting like this early in the morning, my son? Where are you two going?'

But he did not seem to care. He still held his wife's hand and walked towards the backyard. His mother felt her heart thumping. Her son had never defied her before. She had chosen her daughter-in-law herself and now it seemed she was going to pay a price for it. She repeated,

'Do you hear what I am saying? Where are you taking her?'

He stopped suddenly. He turned to look at his mother. He went on looking at her. He had never uttered a strong word directly to his mother. He could not remember his father who had left this world when he was still very young. His mother was everything to him. He let go his wife's hand and came to stand near his mother, facing her.

'Why didn't you come out like this yesterday, Ma? Why didn't you stand in front of me? Why didn't you tell me, don't beat her anymore, otherwise she'll die? Why did you all hide inside the room and close your eyes? Look for once at her back. It looks like a field that has been just ploughed. If once, at least once, you had bothered to see...' He could not continue any more. He hugged his mother and like a little child started crying uncontrollably.

His mother hated to see a man cry. Was she now the mother of a hen-pecked husband? The very thought made her bow her head in shame. She pushed him away, still weeping, and said sharply, 'You have beaten your own wife, why should we interfere? If you are so fond of her, why did you thrash her in front of others?'

So, this was how his mother saw it. He felt stricken. He was too weak. He wiped his tears with his calloused palms and said, 'All right, then don't try to prevent us from going now too. And don't try to block my way and ask where I am taking her.'

Both husband and wife walked together across the now sunlit courtyard. She looked back at her mother-in-law. Perhaps she did not understand the begging look in her daughter-in-law's eyes. The sisters-in-law did not understand why, despite her husband holding her hand, she looked back at them. They could only see the pair holding hands and the pile of work in the kitchen that was waiting for them.

As she walked ahead, she touched her husband's naked arm with her free hand. She tried not to think of the work left behind. She tried to concentrate on only one thing – she was going to do something she had never done before – sharing the work with her husband. Their back garden would be filled with Kakini *tamul* saplings. They would grow into graceful trees and the bunches of areca nuts would decorate their tops. The thought of the areca nut bunches made her young body tremble with anticipation. She said a silent prayer 'O God! Let my mother-in-law live well and long to enjoy the *tamul* from her garden. Keep her healthy for a long, long time.'

The Bhuichampa Flower

Ruplekha Devi

I sit on the steps of Na-math (steps) leading up from the temple courtyard. I look down, mesmerised. It is a busy afternoon and crowds are milling but this corner is away from the hullabaloo. You can afford to lose yourself in the quiet atmosphere. Despite the cacophony of sounds down below, you can indulge in introspection here, and perhaps confide in the Mother of fear, regret, death and salvation. And wonder at the vagaries of life – the search for happiness, enjoyment of earthly pleasures, lust and desire.

Why not? After all, this temple is devoted to Devi Kamakhya whom the people worship to fulfill their desires.

Original Title: Bhuichampa

Durga puja is round the corner. The compound has been cleared of weeds and unwanted creepers. Garlands of marigold and tuberose and little triangular flags in red, blue and saffron announcing the great prowess of the Devi are fluttering in the soft breeze. Some corners of the area display arcades made of flowers and bouquets. Along with the local foliage, I can also see foreign flowers like orchids. The old and the modern merge together. The ambience is of anticipation, satisfaction and hope.

The noise of the festivities has not reached the Namath. I observe the preparations for the coming festival in the temple premises. They seem slothful and soundless from my position here. I feel as if I am watching a silent movie. In front of me is a long line of pilgrims, like a train. From a little baby in somebody's lap to the elderly, people stand in different poses; someone yawns, someone sings a devotional song. People from different corners of the country, perhaps from abroad too, have arrived here. The priests – *pandas* – carry trays of flowers and offerings, looking for devotees. They are negotiating with them about the cost of the puja offerings. The huge goats that roam the ground and the troupes of monkeys look for a chance to snatch the garlands and fruits from the tray of some careless devotee. Yes, I see the earthly beings standing in rows, patiently awaiting a brighter future. I draw myself away from the scene and let my mind roam through waves of consciousness to connect with the goddess. But a refrain of nonsensical sounds disturb me – 'all routes are busy, *sabhi line byost hai kripaya line por rohe ya thori der...'* I am unable to concentrate but try anyway.

A blood-red saree *aanchal* brushes past me as if blown by a stormy wind. Is it an illusion, sleep-induced image, or have I established a connection with the goddess, I wonder. A 440-volt spark descending from the wires – golden sparks – shining. What was that? Is it a ray of sunshine filtering through the tree branches seeking to reach the sanctum sanctorum of the *devipith*? A ray piercing through the branches of the ancient peepul tree now blinds my eyes.

I rub my eyes. What happened? Suddenly, I become aware of the surroundings. My ears are assailed by the chant of the Gayatri Mantra being broadcast through the loudspeakers. Too much sweet can be like poison, nauseating. Just a few years ago it was a secret mantra, which the priest whispered in the ear of the newly initiated boy with the sacred thread – a mantra strong and rich. But now look at its degradation, a public demonstration that has lost its aura.

Is someone weeping? Or am I mistaken? I have seen many with their cheeks stained with tears, overwhelmed by the aura as they stand in front of the goddess. Now, like a radar, I turn my neck from side to side to check the source of the sound. Well, I discover the source. It is the weeping of a new bride!

Ha, ha, ha! Perhaps she has just got married in the temple, or is about to be. Marriage – *biya* – a short word but with myriad meanings. For a girl, it is the occasion of a lifetime when she puts her future in the hands of someone in complete faith. I often wonder why these girls don't try to make their own destiny rather than decide to offer everything in their possession to some stranger. Odd. At this important moment, I don't see anyone with this weeping girl, no woman friend, no relative. She is wearing a bright red saree, her head covered by a veil of net and crowned by a white tiara made of the dried water-plant Kuhila.

I observe her silently. My restless eyes stray to her, ignoring the attractive scenes of the festivities around the temple. Whether you know her or not, a bride somehow always attracts you like a magnet. My eyes send signals to the brain. Her nose... her figure… her dress... the presence of relatives... her social status... mental condition... financial status... etc., etc. Her complexion is the hue of a catfish, but her face and eyes are bright. People say that a would-be bride looks beautiful in any case. She wears a nose-pin, a cheap necklace adorns her young neck, her wrists show off colourful glass bangles. She smells of raw tea leaves. Yes, she is from the tea garden, definitely. Two silver anklets encircle her feet. Her limbs are still too thin for a mature girl. Why is she getting married at such a young age? Where is she from? How cruel are her parents to marry her off at this age when the flower is yet to bloom fully, I wonder.

As these thoughts churn in my mind, a man appears at the scene. He is wearing a kurta-pajama and is carrying a crown made of white Kuhila. So this is her groom! He sits on a step and mumbles something grimly. The girl looks unhappy. Then she wails loudly. I shift my eyes from them. Nothing new there. The usual tiff between two lovers.

The *panda* in his red attire approaches them and shouts angrily. 'Oi, oi, Nimu! Come here. Let me see if I can do something. You nincompoop, you bring an under-age girl and then even reveal her true age! How can I manage to have the marriage registered now? You stupid man, why couldn't you increase her age by two years? Would it have reduced your wife's price, you bastard?'

In his hand are two pretty garlands and a tray of fruits which would have been an offering to the goddess. The three of them rush towards the temple. Now I understand what is happening. It is a case of abduction and that too of an under-age girl. If the girl is below 18 years, the temple authorities cannot enter the couple's name in the marriage register. They have to have the registration done first and only then can the temple wedding ceremonies be performed.

Times have changed indeed. In the olden days, if you took a vow in front of the goddess, it was taken for granted that the couple would stay together through thick and thin no matter what. Never would they dare to defy the vow taken in front of the Goddess Kamakhya as witness and ever think of a separation.

A marriage is meant to be a relationship that continues through seven births. These days even before the wedding day is over, conflicts break out. Sometimes the *pandas* even have to be in the witness box in the court. The temple authorities are accused of compliance, and indirectly, even the goddess, for recognising the wedding rituals. Often gangs entice girls with promises, organise a sham wedding and then traffic them to another state. Some men marry, become the fathers too, but do not give the woman the status of a wife. They may even drive away the woman. After all, she cannot furnish proof of her marriage which was performed secretly, and away from her social circle. She cannot claim any damages either. These days the temple authorities go strictly by the government rule. Good, very good!

Once the curiosity about this case is satiated , my senses – eyes, nose, ears – return to my body silently. I close my eyes and evoke a mantra dedicated to Goddess Kamakhya:

Kamakhyang kama sampurnnang kameshwaring harapriyam.

Kamanang dehime nitong kameswari nomohostute

(Devi Kamakhya, wife of Kameswar, beloved of Hara

Who fulfills all our desires, to Her I pray every day)

Ah, the goddess' image dominates my mind... she who rides the lion... bedecked with lotus flowers... I worship you with five lamps... and with the bell in my left-hand ringing... I move my tongue to ululate, making the traditional welcoming sound. The conch shell, bells, cymbals all orchestrate together to spread the message of happiness and good fortune. I offer flowers and sandalwood paste. I spray perfumed *attar*. Ah, the perfumed air... the smell of joss sticks and incense... my ears take in the soothing mantras and chanting in a deep voice...

Krite kormoni sidhyate kamonashu sureswari totu
martyah kamrupmiti rupam kalpayat...

(In this holy *pith* whoever prays to Devi Sureswari,
his wish is fulfilled. So people come to this land they
call Kamrup…

How beautiful she is... the Mahamaya... my heart fills up... I bow, stretching on the ground. I am now trying to reach her feet… chanting... *Rupang dehi... jayangdehi... yoshu dehi...*

(Grant me grace…Grant me success…Grant me esteem…)

Thap… thap… thap…

Somebody is touching my head. Is it the goddess

herself? How fortunate I am to be blessed by the Mother like this!

'Oi, Mastoroni!' the middle-aged woman addresses me as a teacher, alluding to my profession.

'Why are you sitting in a trance like this on the Namath stairs and at midday too?' She continues, 'If you have finished visiting the temple, come have lunch with me.'

'No, not today. I have some chores to finish. I'll come another day. It's time to go back to Guwahati.'

The woman who had barged into my thoughts moves away. I was on the verge of flying into another sphere and she broke into it. Fie, this rude present!

I see the couple in the temple ground again. Like the *gandharva bibaha* way of marriage in ancient times we hear about, exchanging flower garlands and cutting a raw banana into two, they too have become man and wife, I surmise. Now the *panda* must have sent them to do the *parikrama,* the ritualistic walk around the temple. Yes, yes, I am right. Look at them, holding hands, walking together shyly! Ah, how romantic!

My curiosity almost overtakes me. I feel like running down the stairs and shouting, 'Wah, wah! The wedding is done! It's over!' I don't know why, even at this age when I have witnessed so much, my inner core is still a bit naive.

At last the wait is over. The bride sits not far from me.

'So, you are married now?'

'*Ha, hoi gelek,*' she replies in the typical language

spoken in the local tea gardens Yes, it's done.'

'Your name?'

'Champa.'"

'Where's your house?'

'Dolapur tea garden.'

'And the groom's house?'

'In *desh*. In the country.'

'What does it mean, *desh*?'

'His home is far from here.'

'Ok, I understand. Nobody has come with you?'

'No, no one. *Moi eklai aahili* – I have come alone.'

'Who is there at home?'

I have unearthed all about Champa. Her father is a labourer at the Dolapur tea estate. Her mother works as a domestic help in the garden manager's bungalow. Her elder sister also works there. Her younger brother goes to school. At other times, he loiters around with his friends. Her mother does not allow her to go to school and compels her to work at a nearby bungalow. She scolds her when she refuses to go there. But Champa hates those chores. Her mother does not approve of her running around among the tea bushes or playing on the swing under the Kadam tree. And if she ever saw her having a bath in the little spring near the garden, which she did sometimes, she would kill her. Champa was also scared of the sahibs and memsahibs of the bungalow. If she makes a mistake, however small, they beat her up.

To get away from all this, she has run away with Nimu. He used to visit Haria *kaka (*uncle) often. That's where they exchanged glances. So when he proposed, she decided to leave with him without telling anyone at home. She knew her mother would not have allowed her to marry him. Her elder sister has yet to get married. Today they would leave for Nimu's home in the village far from here. She is not worried that the temple did not allow them to get the marriage registered. Now that she is married to Nimu, it won't be a sin to live with him, right?

Champa looks at me for support. She looks so happy, hopeful about the new life. I look at her kohl-lined bright eyes, the small nose-pin, the big red bindi on her forehead and the smooth dark skin. 'Yes,' I say but I hesitate. An innocent face, a girl who has just crossed adolescence, unaware of the complexities of the outside world.

'How do I look, didi?' she asks me.

'You are a very beautiful girl, Champa.'

'Ha, ha, ha! Nimu says the same thing.' She giggles.

'Oh, you *pagli* (mad) girl!'

'I am telling you the truth.'

'Ha, ha, ha!' I join her in her happy laughter. Her unbridled joy touches me.

But the mind is a treacherous thing. Even amidst this joy something lurks in my consciousness, a fear of the unknown, an apprehension. Somehow a verse of Jigar

Moradabadi escapes my lips,

Yeh Ishq Nahi Aasan bus itna samajh lijiye
Aik Aag Ka Darya Hai aur Doob Kar Jana Hai

To love is not easy, just try to understand
It's a river of fire and you have to swim in it

****

Today is the second day of the Ambubachi festival at the Kamakhya temple. Like a river in spate after incessant rain, people have been streaming into the temple. Nature has been playing hide and seek with the sun and rain in this month of Ashar. Undeterred, lakhs of people from all corners of the country have been congregating at Nilachal hill. They have settled down wherever possible – in the temple compound, around the smaller temples of *dasa-mahavidya* dedicated to the ten incarnations of the Goddess Kali, in the caves of the hills. Crowds of ascetics and sadhus in exotic garb of red, black or in wraps imitating the spotted tiger skin, are everywhere. Some of them are almost naked; some wear only a minimal strip of cloth round the torso. Some have covered their bodies with ash, while some have rubbed perfumed sandalwood paste all over. If somebody's preference is for the blue colour, somebody else has covered himself in yellow powder and also draped himself in yellow clothes in obeisance to Lord Krishna. Again, some others have smeared vermillion all over the body like the stone statues lining the temple's exterior. In another corner, the sadhus who have taken a vow of silence mumble mantras while counting the beads of the *jopmala* (rosaries). At the junction of the lanes, a group of sadhus sing *bhajans* in praise of the goddess. To attract attention, some even dance or show off their sleight of hand, while some give lectures on religion. In short, each person or a group tries to outdo each other.

It has been raining the whole day. *Ambu* means water and *bachi* means cascading water. In short, the word Ambubachi has kept up its reputation today. Holding an umbrella over my head, I roam among the groups of ascetics. It is so crowded that there is not even room to stand. I feel a wave of people sweep me away. I observe one ascetic opening his coiled bun and spreading his long hair on the path to draw attention. Another has been in the *Sirsasana* yoga pose for hours. Many colours, many scenes – they are changing constantly. This is, after all, the famous annual Ambubachi mela of the Kamakhya temple.

The air is pervaded by a sharp odour. It is not the fetid smell emanating from a mixture of rainwater, fruits, flowers, lighted joss sticks and day-old food. Looking for the source of the reeking smell that irritated my nose, I reach a group of ascetics sitting in a circle, and puffing from the *chillum*. The smoke rises in vertical rings into the air around them. Their eyes are glazed.

A couple of them shout from time to time... *bom, bom, Bholanath* as if to announce that they are awake. Not far from them is a young woman dressed like Goddess Kali. A crowd of people stood around her. She is wearing a vermillion-red saree, a bunch of strings of *rudrakh* beads hungfrom her neck, a golden tiara crowned her head and in her left hand she held a trident. She looked at the palms or the lines on forehead of a person and was saying something incessantly. Some of those who consulted her smiled in happiness while others looked worried. Suddenly she seemed to fall into a spell. She turned her head round and round, her hair flying in all directions and started screaming loudly. Immediately a few ascetics who were sitting next to her started strumming the manjira and singing a devotional song. After some time, as the dance reached a crescendo, a sanyasi sprinkled some water on her from his brass jug. The passion slowly disappeared from the woman's body. She sat down calmly in her corner as before. People in the know knew that all this drama was a trick to attract people.

I left the place to check out what else awaited me. It seemed that the devotees did not bother about the mud or dirt on the ground. Without going into serious discourses on the influence of religion on humans, it was humbling to feel that since ancient times human imagination has helped to craft a world of creation and reproduction. As the belief goes, this female deity, Kamakhya, meaning nature, was menstruating during the Ambubachi. After a few days she would be pregnant and give birth to lush rice fields, fruits and animals. We are all the children of Mother Earth. How opulent was this imagination!

Sometimes I wonder, what drives these people to tolerate such discomfort, such difficulties to journey to this temple, year after year? Is it to give themselves freely to a greater power and then attain salvation? Or pray for worldly goods? I have asked many visitors through the years as I visit the temple during this time. Many answered that the search for the almighty was never-ending. So, they travel from one pilgrimage centre to another, keeping track of the festivals at each of them. In short, the festivals in the country decided their calendar for the year. They also enjoy lots of doles. They do not need to buy railway tickets; they do not need the luxury of rooms to sleep in, or partake of sumptuous food. They take to this life of an itinerant willingly, roaming and sleeping wherever they land. What an adventurous life, I often think. After the Kamakhya festival, many will leave for the Bolebom festival in Bihar. And life goes on like this – no worries, no tension, no apprehension. In this journey they find companions on the same wavelength, they marry, have children, the old die and a new generation takes over. A new life is born, continuing the tradition for ages and ages.

Among the thousands congregating at the Ambubachi mela, the face of the woman playing the role of Goddess Kali surfaced in my mind again and again. Why, why? I asked myself. Was I getting drawn into the web of illusion that she had created? No, it couldn't be. Absurd. At least I didn't want to know my future with her help. But, why did I get the feeling that I was close to her? Why did I feel that I knew her? A little disoriented, I walked away from there and went towards the spot where the animal sacrifice was going on.

I found that the so-called Goddess Kali character was taking a break too. She had stopped her theatrical performance for the time being and was resting. The old sadhu was busy collecting the coins that people had given them. I observed her from the corner of my eye. Why did she look vaguely familiar? I look at her eyes lined with kohl, her smooth dark skin, her tiny nose-pin. Where, oh where had I met her before? I just couldn't place her. I was disappointed at my failed memory. I had to admit to myself that my brain was not as sharp as before. With heavy steps I got ready to leave the place.

'Didi, *hei mastoroni*, didi, don't you recognise me?'

I stopped uncertainly in my tracks. Did she know me? She was leaning on a pillow but now she got up and came towards me.

'*Mastoroni-didi*, you couldn't recognise me? Remember we met here on my wedding day, about 10-

12 years ago? Don't you recall? You told me again and again that without registration, getting married was risky. They aren't treated well. I am Champa, Champa of the Dola tea garden... remember now?'

Of course! 'But Champa... oh yes, but how can you be Kali Ma?'

My mouth fell open in astonishment. She caught hold of my hand and led me through the crowd of people who gave way immediately. I followed her, mesmerised. We both reached the stairwell of Na-math and like that day, a decade or so ago, started talking to each other. The noise of the crowd was forgotten and we were absorbed with each other.

I looked at her. That adolescent girl, soft and pliant, the girl from the two-leaves-and-a-bud country, was now adorning this ferocious avatar of Kali-Ma. What had life taught her that she had become old before her time? The alarm bells that rang in my head that day had proved correct, after all. I had again made a mistake. Knowing everything I had still closed my eyes. Unforgiving regret filled my heart.

Even before I asked her, Champa started telling me her story of transformation from an innocent girl from the tea gardens into Kali-ma, as if she was waiting to blurt it all out, something she had kept dammed up in her heart till now.

Nimu, the man who had married her, first took her

to Kolkata and then Delhi. His business was actually as a truck owner. Their conjugal life started on the road in the truck. In Kolkata, she was dumped in a filthy room in a slum. The love story where they lived happily ever after did not really happen. Not even a fortnight had passed before Nimu revealed his true nature. When he did not go out with the truck he would drink the whole day and torture her physically. She had to bear it as she did not know anyone in the city. She learnt to accept that men were like that. Since childhood she had seen how her father and other men created a ruckus after going on a drinking spree with local brew *haria*. But Nimu's drunkenness and the torture were of a different kind.

One night he had brought along six or seven of his friends. They drank heavily, apparently to celebrate their wedding. That night Champa's life changed forever. After that, she was like a corpse. Her so-called husband had offered his young wife to his cronies as if she were a toy. All her dreams were shattered. Disillusioned, she cried inconsolably but it was the last time.

Once the wounds on her body healed, she rebelled. The drunkard could not manage her and took her to Delhi and bargained with a woman to keep her there for three years. In his language, it was called a lease. Champa had heard the word in the garden but it had to do with land, a water-body or something without life. This was the first time that she learnt that in this cruel world people were also leased out. Humans were bought and sold like cows and goats. She was supposed to be a mare that could not be leashed. So she had to be sent to another place in order to be tamed.

The hyenas feasted on her body. The days did not end, the nights were endless, the torture unimaginable. They did not leave any stone unturned to break her physically and mentally. In the secret world of the whorehouse, there were other girls, all abandoned like her. Every day, every night, she felt like a candle, slowly burning and dying. The only thing that kept her alive was waiting for the moment when she could take revenge on that demon, Nimu.

At last that opportunity arrived. After three years, her so-called husband turned up to take her back. Shamelessly he counted the money he had earned from selling the body of the woman he had once accepted as his wife by putting vermillion on her head in the temple. A road trip again, from the hellhole of Delhi to the hellhole in Kolkata. Champa was tired, very tired, mentally and physically. But before life ebbed away, she had one job to finish, her revenge. That kept her alive.

Once they entered West Bengal, Nimu and his assistant got down to have dinner at a dhaba. Champa pretended to be asleep. Taking this opportunity she ran away to another dhaba by the roadside. With all her savings and ornaments she bought a death weapon to destroy Nimu.

A drunk Nimu drove away in the truck of which brakes had been tampered with. Perhaps he thought she was lying under the blanket. It was the end of the inauspicious star that had blackened her life. Champa was free from slavery.

But could even a 'free' woman be free after all? She roamed the jungles, villages and towns looking for shelter. She had nothing to lose. But can a person stop caring for oneself until death takes over? Eventually, she took shelter in a temple in a nondescript village in Bengal. Not far from it was a temple of Goddess Dakshina Kali. During the day people came to offer prayers but at night there was a deathly silence. The head of the temple was an old sadhu. He was ready to offer her a roof over her head. But in exchange for what? She realised long ago that the protector often turned out to be a devourer. She judged the situation on the scale of bitter experience and accepted the offer without protesting. She decided it was better to be a chattel to a priest than be a prostitute.

'*Oi mastoroni*, what are you talking about with the Kali-ma? Are you asking when you'd get married? Ha, ha, ha!'

The voices of the familiar women from Kamakhya *dham* brought me back to my surroundings. Both of us had tears in our eyes. Two hours had passed. I had forgotten the time and place while I was talking with Champa.

'Champa, I realise what you have gone through. But why have you decided to take on this role as Kali-ma?' I asked.

'This is the best thing that has happened to me. It's due to the blessing of Devi-ma,' she said and then laughed loudly, her outburst mysterious and sarcastic. She continued her story with new energy.

It was the annual puja of Goddess Kali. There was a huge *puja* arranged by the villagers with fruit *prasad* and lunch distributed free to everybody. The grounds of the temple reverberated with the beating of the drums, cymbals and the sonorous *kalia* trumpet. Champa was busy helping with the arrangements. Suddenly something happened. The sounds bored into her head and she started swinging rhythmically with the beat. Then she started shouting loudly. Her hair, which was tied in a neat bun, became loose. She breathed fast. A few men forcefully tried to make her sit down and sprinkled water on her face and eyes. It failed to calm her down. She felt as if her whole body was filled with endless energy, an unearthly force. She snatched the trident from the image of Kali and started dancing furiously. The people were aghast and shouted, 'She is under the spell of Kali-ma, the goddess has entered her body. *Jai Ma Kali*!' They bowed their heads in reverence. Even the old sadhu, who had exploited her, trembled in fear and bowed at her feet. A few in the crowd asked her questions. Whether with the knowledge culled from her experiences or some unexplained power that came over her, she answered them.

This was a new Champa, her new avatar as the powerful, angry Kali-ma. Now she was the one who ruled over the Kali temple in the village and the old sadhu was her savant. Champa had turned into a powerful, arrogant, vengeful woman.

'But how can you spend the rest of your life wearing this mask? If you so desire you can leave this play-acting and start a new life. I'll help you, Champa,' I offered.

'Why do I need a new life? My new life started a few years ago. I am happy now. Now the men touch my feet in fear and reverence. I am Kali after all, who stood on the chest of God Shiva, her husband. I am all powerful. I lost everything in your modern world. Now the old, ancient world has given me back everything – as a woman, as a source of energy, I am worshipped and respected. I am happy in the old world. I don't want anything to do with your modern life. We will meet again, *mastoroni-didi*. You keep well. If I am alive, I will see you again,' she said.

Champa hugged me long. Then with the huge trident in her hand held aloft, she quickly went down the steps of Na-math. People made way for her. It was like a scene from some mythical time, the goddess coming down to earth to kill a demon who harassed the people. I smiled, but with a trace of sadness.

The Marketplace

Gayatri Doley

The month of *fagun* is already here. Let it come. This year, the winter has not been that harsh. I am not sure if the last bite of the cold season is still here, or has already gone. I know that spring is waiting on the threshold, ready to make an appearance any day. And then will come the hot season, followed by the monsoon. Let them arrive at will, as they wish. The seasons come and go in succession leaving their mark on the skin, the body. Look at the dust storm swirling around now – spreading a canopy over the houses and the roads, hiding them from view. I can't make out the contours of the faces of people passing by. Perhaps they too can't recognise me. I often cover my head with a blue scarf. Some of them,

Original Title: Bazaar

who had not seen me or pretended not to, have no option but to come nearer to this corner when lashed by the dust storm. To be honest, they don't come to meet me but to take shelter in the empty patch of land next to my place. Where else would they find a corner like this where they are able to stand undisturbed? Let them.

Digambar is not open today. You ask, 'What do you mean?' Why, it's the shop across the road that sells clothes. They say, he sells 'branded' clothes. It's quite successful, it seems. People who are not known for any achievement but want to flaunt themselves as a 'brand' want to wear branded clothes. Ha, ha, ha! You know what's so funny? Even the brands have imitations, that is, there are fake brands. But then there are people who knowingly look for fake brands. People come to Digambar and ask for a fake pair of Adidas sneakers or a Levi's pair of jeans. I wonder sometimes, are there fake copies of people too? At times, Digambar convinces the customer that the fake brand is actually a genuine one and makes a good profit. The customer flaunts it proudly while walking out of the shop. To tell the truth, it's difficult to differentiate between the fake and the real. The customer who asks for the fake version of a brand, is he himself a fake person? Or take Digambar, for example. When he convinces the customer that the fake version is actually a genuine brand, does it prove that he himself is a fake? Anyway, in short, Digambar sells both fakes and genuine brands.

This season also means that young girls get excited at the prospect of getting married. As also do the prospective grooms. In front of Bakul, the furniture shop, you will see a line of parents with worry lines on their foreheads. At other times, you can make out the owner Ujjal's face in the dark only with the help of a candle, but now his face looks quite attractive, brightened by all this business. He is regarded as being rather hoity-toity and so the envious in the neighbourhood have been instructed to keep him under surveillance. They keep tabs on how many bedsteads for the trousseau have gone out of the shop, and how many brown-coloured showcases along with steel almirahs. Quite a lot, frankly. I must say that those who have kept an eye on him have done their duty faithfully. In any case, our eyes work very well when we want to find fault with others.

When these various furniture pieces leave the premises of Bakul's shop, an unpleasant smell pervades the air. The shop's name, Bakul, refers to the heady aroma of the flower with the same name but it has never been able to entice me though I have been familiar with the scent for many years. I prefer the smell of the Champa flower, though truthfully, I have never come across it. (Let me whisper a secret in confidence: Do I hate the Bakul flower's smell for a special reason? Am I jealous of the bridal bed? I imagine it, away from prying eyes. The room, the blue bed sheet, the two soft cotton-wool pillows, its covers embroidered with flowers, like the ones I crafted after my matriculation exam. They are still there, packed away somewhere. As I watch, the bedstead leaves in a Tata Tempo van. The tyres make a screeching sound, and I fall off the imaginary bed. I fall so hard that it hurts my chest. But I don't tell anyone and join the other pairs of eyes observing the assembly of vehicles loaded with furniture leaving for different destinations from Bakul. Suddenly, I wonder, are there other eyes which are keeping a watch on me too? Because, like a leafless tree that even the wild *fagun* month air can't shake, I keep sitting here. Perhaps that's why I hate it even more. Like the dark-complexioned owner is called Ujjal, which means bright. does the fact that this shop is called Bakul that makes me hate the smell of the flower? Otherwise, who can dislike the sweet scent of the Bakul flower?

I must mention another outlet that I hate equally. Sopun Beauty Parlour, which sells *sopun* or dreams to women. Even fifteen years ago, the eyebrows of women of this town or their hair were tended by the women themselves. Then some girl from the other side of the river eloped with a boy from this side of the bank. We heard she had taken a course on threading eyebrows and cutting hair. She was the one who opened the parlour. At first, the girls visited it surreptitiously. I never went there myself, though. Very soon, glass-fronted beauty parlours sprung up in other parts of the town. Inside, the owners with their short, styled hair sat proprietarily.

Sabitri too of Sopun Beauty Parlour. During the festivals like Bihu, Durga Puja, etc., the crowds would throng the Sopun Parlour. The women at the parlour would labour over the customers' hair through the day and send them back satisfied. Some came to get their hair cut, some to straighten their hair. Some came to show off their hair or get it cut in layers, which I hear, is called a Step Cut. Funnily, in the olden days if thieves got caught, they were given the same kind of haircut. Then there is a style of haircut, which seems to be singed with fire and which I learnt, is called a Razor Cut. The girls and women come out from the Sopun Beauty Parlour like a group of galloping horses with their 'thief cut', 'full cut, 'horse cut', etc.

Perhaps, I am thinking about this too much or saying too much. However, it's normal that I do that. Or I think too much. People have accepted that I do so. In fact, if I don't, people would look at me in astonishment as if I were out of sync.

Till yesterday, Sabitri, the owner of Sopun Beauty Parlour, had been regarded as a very lucky lady. Her face was like the *chou* in the paddy field, bright and eye-catching, placed there to ward off the black eye, as if conveying the message: 'Don't envy my wealth' or 'Don't envy my good luck', etc. But look at what happened! Her husband apparently set his eyes on a woman who has never lined her eyes with kajol, never even put a puff of powder on her face, and she coils her hair into an old-fashioned bun. That lady has become his lover. At first, no one could believe it. How could they? Wasn't he the epitome of a caring husband? He used only the fondest terms to address Sabitri – O, my *Janmoni*, O my *Sonmoni* – my heart, my golden girl. And now? When she was busy giving shape to the dreams of other women with facials that gave them a special glow, threading their eyebrows to achieve that perfect arch, cutting their hair in different styles to suit their faces, her own dreams were shattered.

Frankly, I am not that sorry about it. The way she and the other women walked past me, flaunting their 'parloured' bodies, it seemed as if, I was their Enemy No. 1. Ha, ha! And now? What do they say now?

There are a couple more shops next to my place. One serves sweets and tea. Another is a *paan-bhandar*, selling areca nuts and betel leaves. They are okay. They are on good terms with me. Sometimes I get a gut feeling that the one selling paan looks into my eyes rather deeply. Somewhere a string, as if in a sitar, trembles with the faintest sound. But I have kept it to myself.

Some people get curious and ask the shopkeepers about me. Some volunteer information. I can see it by the look in their eyes. Whatever they want to know, let them try to find out. But I look out for the ones who show pity. Because my situation is pitiable. I have been sitting under this shed for years, through the hot and cold seasons. Enjoyment of life, of colour and music, they are all strangers to me. Isn't it sad that a young woman sitting under a crumbled shed has lost all ability to enjoy life? Perhaps I could have had something of my own, a little colour, a little happiness, if things were different.

Here comes Jadumoni Hazarika with his signature loping gait. I pretend not to see him. He looks at me. He is also looking at the house looming over mine. His house. Everybody knows that he can't stand the sight of me. He knows that I can't bear the sight of him either.

Readers, till now, I have written little about myself. But by now you must have guessed a bit about me. I have described some people around me, the shops, etc., so that you get an idea about my situation. My other concern is that the writer of this story should not give the wrong impression about me. Sure, as a writer she has the right to paint me in her own way. But, however colourful an image she wants to project about me, I have told you in the beginning that I am like a leafless, dry tree standing alone that even the wild *fagun* wind cannot muzzle. I am in the habit of gossiping about others and tend to plead my own case favourably. I suppose you are a bit bored listening to me. Anyway, when you will read about me next as described by the writer, please try not to forget what I have told you, because that's who I am.

Now writer, carry on! I will sit here without interfering in your work.

The first thing to do now is to give a name to the character. It's not wise to use the real name because all the things she has said are true and also about her character as also Jadumoni Hazarika's. It's also true that she has been sitting like this, alone, year after year, never mind the dust storms or the pouring rain. Characters who entered her life have now all disappeared, that's also true. And, since all these things are true about her, there is a need to find a fictitious name for her.

It's not going to be Madhubala, Madhuri, Kajol, Deepika or Katrina – they are all famous actresses. Then who? Could it be Jeuti, Seuti, Malati, Tagar – typical Assamese names? Not really. Those names won't suit her character. Jetuki, then? But that sounds like the name of a married woman. She is not married, and the possibility that she will get married on some future date is uncertain too. Tagar? Like the mature heroine in Bina Baruah's book *Jibonor Baatot*, whom Kamalakanta cheated? The woman who could not reveal the shame because of societal norms? No. Tagar won't suit her either. She is not as forgiving or generous.

But we have to find a name. If we go on like this, we will never finish this story. So, for the sake of convenience, without much more examination, without going too deep into the meaning, let's settle for Dhananti. Ok, that's decided. Dhananti. (Just rambling)

Dhananti cannot keep her mouth shut. It's not

important as to when she learnt to utter the harsh words. More importantly, why did she have to learn them? A decade or so earlier, her way of talking was not like this acidic and without frills for certain. Today, she is so unrelenting and vicious that others do not dare approach her. Only a sentry like Dhananti can utter such words without a care. There is another reason: she doesn't have any fear. Rather she is worried that one day, due to circumstances, she will lose the urge to speak these vile words, however unwillingly spoken. In fact, these words have helped her to stick to this bedraggled place.

The vigil has been going on forever for a patch of land measuring only eight sq. feet. Next to it stands the tall building belonging to Jadumoni Hazarika, her uncle, her father's arrogant younger brother. He had proposed that a building be constructed on the elongated plot belonging to her. Dhananti's eight-feet of living quarters would be a part of it. She would receive a handsome one-time payment as compensation. What was the use of even one foot of land to a spinster? Till she lived she would live off her father and then, her brother. After that – finished. So what's the point of her holding on to the plot of land?

But why should Dhananti accept it? She doesn't beg for favours from anyone and makes a living by selling stationery from her own shop. She values her independence. So, never!

Advice.

Enticement.

Scolding. Threats.

Warning.

No! No! No! She won't allow it.

That was the final answer from her.

Her good-for-nothing father Bholou had readily accepted the offer from his younger brother. What's the problem, he had argued. At least, they would receive something from him. Her drunkard brother had also conceded. He could ensure his liquor supply for a while without much effort with that money.

But Dhananti was adamant. She would never sell the plot.

Her grandfather had left behind a huge plot of land for his four sons to be divided equally. Jadumoni Hazarika had made good use of his share by building houses everywhere: his own house, houses for rent, sheds for shops. Her lazy father had sold block after block of his own share to his enterprising brother without telling her.

At first, when Jadumoni Hazarika piled stone-chips and sand next to the *kaccha* foundation of their house. Dhananti was told that he was going to build a house for all of them. She was very happy and shared the good news with everybody in the neighbourhood. They would stay on the upper floor. Her uncle's younger son and family would stay on the ground floor. Jadumoni Hazarika would stay in his original house. She had even told them which room she would occupy; how from the balcony she would watch the people going up and down the road.

And then one day Dhananti's dream came crashing down with a loud thud. She found out that Jadumoni Hazarika was negotiating rent with customers even before the construction was complete. So, it was not meant for her or her family, but for strangers who would move in as tenants. She remembered her uncle telling her rudely that if she wanted a flat, she would have to pay in advance.

By this time the building was already coming up next to her stationery stall. Jadumoni Hazarika waited for Dhananti's shop to be demolished; then the rest of the windows, two of them, could be installed.

Windows? He wanted to put in two windows? To look at whom? And where?

No, it wouldn't be allowed. Dhananti would not allow the demolition of her little house and the stall attached to it. She won't let that eight feet patch to be taken over. She didn't want that flat any more. She had long ago given up any hope of sitting in a room with a view and observing people going up and down the road below. Give back the land. Take down the building! Take down!

But the land was long ago registered in Jadumoni Hazarika's name. Her father and her drunkard brother had by now spent all the money they had got for it.

Okay, Dhananti decided. The building would never have a path of approach to the building. And no windows either. Because it was simple. Laying the approach road would not be possible without demolishing her shop. The joke was, if Dhananti didn't relent, the approach road to the building behind could not be built.

It has been three years since the building was completed. Jadumoni Hazarika filed a case in the court against her, alleging encroachment. Dhananti also filed a case against him alleging that he had tried to take away by force her legitimate right over the patch of land.

Both cases have been in the court for three years. If one day Jadumoni Hazarika was called to appear, Dhananti was summoned another day. Jadumoni Hazarika returned from the court with his usual arrogance. And Dhananti returned with hope.

Both of them told their neighbours, the people on the street, 'I will win, you'll see!' The people listened to both of them and decided on their own as to who was right. Both of them searched for the right person to carry the message to the rival. If that person lent a sympathetic ear, he or she was bombarded with all the complaints and resentment against the other.

And it has been going on like this for a long time. Like an eagle following an old cow hoping it will fall down dead any day, both of them have been nursing the hope of winning the case.

The amount of money required to fight the case was huge, Dhananti was told. She had to spend all the money she earned from her stationery shop. Ultimately, she had to shut it down.

Now she sits in a chair in front of the closed shop to guard it. She knows that if he saw no one around, Jadumoni Hazarika would demolish the structure. At night, she forces her father to take her place.

This is what I know about Dhananti. I don't know how to react to her. Looking at her, I am not sure if I tacitly support her, or like most others, look at her askance or with a sense of pity. But yes, I am very, very curious about her.

Is she avaricious? Otherwise, who would have patience to guard a plot just eight sq. feet?

What does she want? To keep alive the memory of her late grandfather or ensure some modicum of respect for her father's legacy? But he had sold off all the land that belonged to him and Jadumoni Hazarika has already registered it in his name. Or is she afraid that with the selling of this plot she will lose the last connection to her family's name?

Why had Dhananti never married? Was there a man in her life? If so, why had she refused to become a wife? Or did her youth pass by as she waited to become the rightful owner of the eight- feet plot of land? These questions have led to worry lines on many a forehead.

Mine too. But Dhananti has asked me to pause here.

Why have I asked the writer to pause? I think she has become too curious about my personal life. These days I get bored with personal details. There is a bazaar out there in the digital world where talk about personal life has a value. What's the use of measuring my happiness, my sorrow, on a scale?

Everybody has a chapter in life hidden somewhere. It emerges from the deep recesses at times to confront the person. I too am tested from time to time as I peep into myself. I see many of the things that have been left unsaid. But people want to know more – to enjoy, to salivate over, to chew on – all those unspoken things. Let them. I keep many things to myself. But this is a bazaar. When there are no customers, people need something to discuss, some subject to ponder over. If it is a little salacious, all the better, so that it can be whispered among the group. If one of them is able to convey a sense of sadness, the listener might even offer tea and paan for free. But if the story is dry, without any interesting tidbits to add to the gossip, the seller would not spare even ten rupees for a blouse of 2x2 material.

Yes, I have given the writer permission to write my story. But I also know that she won't be able to solve my problem. I am a nonentity in this bazaar. People around me sell things. I have sold all and I am now guarding my own bones. I know I won't be able to carry on this responsibility much longer. My savings have dwindled and I have reached rock bottom. I know it's not possible for a lone woman to keep at bay a person like Jadumoni Hazarika. But I still hope. It keeps me alive, by not giving in.

As I sit here like this, I am not sure what you wanted to know about me. Even the writer, though she empathises with me, is unable to draw a true picture. She herself is rather moody and adamant. So, I know that once she has been stopped from writing further, she will never write about me again. So I shall have to paint my own portrait and finish the job.

I am a still figure. For the last three years I have been sitting on the same bench thinking the same thoughts.

I as a writer have some thoughts too though I don't know if they are right.

I had selected the character of Dhananti without any particular reason. But I can't express in a few sentences the culmination of her character, with a plus or minus, because she is still sitting the same way, in the same place, and for the same reason. So, if I suddenly cut her off midway as a character, she will be very hurt. I know she will never read this story. But just because I can understand her pain, I should not mould her character in the way I want just for the sake of the story. So here, at this moment, I am leaving Dhananti as a character in the bazaar.

Among many things on sale in the bazaar, Dhananti's

dream, her life, are in the market too but with a character of its own, something living.

Aren't we objects in the bazaar too?

Nobody knows who is waiting for whom and why.

Dhananti is waiting. We are waiting.

Life is a horse-drawn buggy that continues on its way despite having to pause at times.

Dunoi

Kavyashree Mahanta

It was his eldest sister's wedding day. It was not a big affair with a pandal and feast for the whole village, but a small one as befits a farmer's family. He was seven or eight years old then. He was very close to his sister. His older brother and two other sisters always tormented him. So he avoided them. His eldest sister was not like that. However much he howled, even with his nose streaming with snot, she kept him close to her. His mother hardly had time to spare after completing her household chores. When he was with this sister he felt secure and safe as if he were with his mother.

She would feed him pods of jackfruit, slices of guava or would take him for a walk on the village road.

Original Title: Dunoi

He was rather scared of his father. If he heard him scold one of his siblings, he would start to wail in fear.

And now his favourite sister was getting married. He moped as he could not stay close to her. To top it all, the invitees teased him mercilessly when they saw him. The boys who were older to him pulled down his half pant to harass him.

He sobbed copiously but the boys found it even more amusing. Hearing him cry, his sister came out of the room and scolded the boys, 'Why are you after him?' But his mother asked her to go back inside; she was the bride after all.

After sometime, his mother and a few women in the village got ready to go to the pond to collect water, as per custom, for the bride's ritual bath. He saw that in a traditional *dunari*, a round tray with a stand and a cover like sieve, rice grains and a few other things were placed. A lighted earthen lamp was also placed in the centre. His mother asked her younger daughter to carry the *dunari*. But he wanted to carry it and started to cry. His mother looked sternly at him but did not say anything. His sister made a face. He threw himself on the floor in a tantrum, shouting and crying at the same time. '*Dunoi..dunoi.. dunoi*,' he cried out, unable to correctly pronounce the word *dunari*. His older brother, sister and other invitees teased him, mimicking him by repeating '*Dunoi..dunoi... dunoi*'. His mother looked at him helplessly and then left to collect water from the village pond with the other women.

Seeing him rolling on the floor, covered in dirt and crying, his sister felt guilty and stopped laughing at him. His father came and reprimanded him severely. He then dragged him to the *dhenki-saal* shed, where the *dhenki,* the wooden foot pestle was kept. He made him sit on a mat on the floor. After some time, he dropped off to sleep but even then he cried out from time to time '*dunoi.. dunoi*'. In the afternoon when the guests arrived, he did not dare to step outside because whoever saw him called out, '*dunoi...dunoi*'. From then on, he was called Dunoi instead of his original name Tutu.

Only his mother and the eldest sister understood him. He conveyed somehow that the rice needed to be mixed with the curry before he ate and that he could not find the *gamosa* (towel) for his bath. When the neighbours asked his sister something or the other, he listened attentively, and tried to repeat the words too. She also talked to him. 'Come, let me fix the pant button.' 'Be careful, don't let it fall.' 'Here, eat this.' He somehow understood what she was saying and when he was hungry, cried out, '*kha.. kha*' (eat, eat).

But strange! When he tried to say something, others either scolded him, or teased him. Slowly he realised that when he cried, the others only laughed at him and so he stopped crying. Instead, he laughed when others laughed. If someone asked him, 'Hei Dunoi, what are you up to?' he smiled and tried to say something. But he found it difficult to pronounce the words he had learnt in his childhood. He never smiled when he saw a girl or a woman. He felt shy and tried to hide from them.

The two sons of his eldest sister whom he loved were now big enough to join in the teasing. His two other sisters were also married. His mother was getting old and was not as active as before. She tried her best to keep him by her side. If she said, 'Go, bring some firewood,' he understood and ran to bring the logs for her. When she went to wash the utensils, he ran with an aluminum bucket to fetch water from the pond. Sometimes in the afternoon when she went to the vegetable patch with a basket and knife, he would immediately bring out the forked stick from the roof of the granary. He didn't need to be told, he understood from the smell or the pace of her walk. His mother talked to herself as she walked alongside him. 'Dunoi is not a blockhead; people who say so are the ones who are. Look at how he sat by the bed day and night when his father was seriously ill. Even the day before he died, nobody guessed that he would go so soon, Dunoi sat near him throughout the night without even blinking.'

His older brother got married a year before his father died. Till then his mother used to serve food to both the brothers together. But lately, his sister-in-law started serving her husband first. Dunoi had lunch with his mother now. His brother worked in a grocery shop in the town. With the approach of autumn, the granary was almost empty. They had to live through the period somehow till the next harvest. His brother's meagre salary would be supplemented by selling vegetables from the kitchen garden. But after his father's death, the kitchen garden lay somewhat neglected. Meanwhile, his sister-in-law's family visited often. They had to be served lunch or dinner, and there was always a shortage of money.

One day, after the last rites of his father's *shraddha were* over, Dunoi's brother told his mother without any forewarning, 'Ask the blockhead to do something. Am I going to feed him all his life?'

His mother was about to serve the pumpkin curry to him. She paused, straightened up and asked, surprised, 'Who? Dunoi?'

'Yes. He is not a baby anymore.'

'But what will he do?' she asked dumbfounded.

'If he can't do anything, let him work as a daily labourer. He can at least hoe the fields, collect the garbage.'

His mother was silent. She had asked herself this question many times without finding an answer. But how could she tell Dunoi to work as a daily labourer? When he was born, there were two granaries full of rice in this house. But marrying off the three daughters meant selling off much of their fertile land. Whatever rice was left was unlikely to last the year.

Dunoi's mother was still battling with the problem. Meanwhile, she tried to teach him to do a few useful chores. She supervised him as he cleared the pond of the moss that covered it by gliding on a *bhoor* (banana stalk boat). She taught him to bind the knots of a bamboo fence and how to trim the tree branches. It was as if his mother had made an agreement with God. Dunoi could not speak and he walked unsteadily. She should be able to make him stand on his feet, before He came calling for her.

One day, Pradip's father who lived two houses away, sent for Dunoi. His mother encouraged him, saying, 'Go! There's no one to look after the kitchen garden in his house. Cows and goats have destroyed his fruit trees and vegetable patches. Go, help him get his garden in order again.'

Dunoi did not need anybody's help. He, on his own, finished the fencing of the two bigha of land within two days. The next day, he gave his mother a hundred rupee note. He was not sure what it was but knew that it was something important and took it home. When his mother took the note and sat stonily, he did not leave her side. He knew very well when her eyes welled up with tears.

One year passed. By now Dunoi became quite skilled at work and worked faster. His arms gained muscle. He could now comprehend the requirements of a job and learnt to prioritise. Sometimes somebody in a household would call out, 'Dunoi, come have some food!' He understood and went to have the meal. If he was asked whether he wanted more, he waved them away. He wanted no more. When he worked he mumbled to himself; sometimes he smiled to himself. All those around him understood him – the sky, the air, the clouds, the leaves on the trees and his mother. Even the bamboo sticks he pushed into the ground to make the fence understood him.

One day, Prasen, Pradip's brother, asked him, 'Dunoi, do you want to go into town with me?'

Prasen had bought a new pick-up van. When he rented out this van, he was also expected to supply the labourers to help in the loading and unloading of the goods. It was difficult to find trustworthy workers in town. Dunoi was good at his work and reliable and so would be of great help. He approached Dunoi's mother with his proposal. She felt uncertain but Prasen persuaded her, 'Bor-ma, you won't be able to look after him all your life. He would be a guard at my shop or garage. If he wants, he can stay there too.'

That convinced her. She always wanted him to have a place of his own. She would not live forever. It was lucky that something like this had come along.

So Dunoi left with two other men in the pick-up van. The two men talked between themselves all the way. Dunoi was busy checking if the things his mother had packed were safely in the bag.

He was given a room behind Prasen's main house. It was arranged that he would have his lunch in the house too. Only in the evening he had to cook some rice on the stove for himself. At first, he did not know how to light the stove and sat uncertainly near it, but soon he learnt to do it too. He even learnt to buy roti from a shed nearby by paying six rupees.

One day, he heard that the buses and vehicles would not ply the next day because of some puja. But Durga Puja was far off. Dunoi did not know the occasion for puja was but saw that the shops were decorated with garlands. Prasen's garage too would hold a puja. Besides the pick-up van, Prasen had an Indica car and a shop for car parts and other paraphernalia. He also had other employees. All of them were busy in preparations for the puja. The whole town seemed to be busy with the festivities. The shops and garages were swept and cleaned and garlands of flowers were hung at the entrances. Strings of lights lit up the evening.

Prasen sent Dunoi on an errand to deliver a few huge cooking pots needed for the feast next day. With Dunoi, a new boy climbed into the pick-up van. Prasen explained to him something in Hindi. The boy smiled at him and they were on their way in the van. It felt nice. The other boys who worked for Prasen talked, shared jokes and news among themselves. Dunoi was not part of their circle. This was a new boy, yet he smiled at him. Dunoi smiled back. The boy asked him something in Hindi. Dunoi did not know the language but knew it was Hindi. He gestured with his head and hands that he didn't know the language. The new boy seemed to understand and shook his head.

The new boy asked him something. Dunoi could understand one word – *kahan*. So, he was asking where his house was. Dunoi could only guess which side his village lay and with his hands he pointed to convey that it was far away. The new boy smiled and seemed to understand. See, Dunoi thought, he has understood me. He wanted to explain more – that from here they had to cross a huge bridge, when the van passed over it there was a *ghrr ghrr* sound, then they would have to wait at the railway crossing; that on the other side there was a big bazaar too. He tried his best and the newfound friend nodded and smiled. Dunoi felt very happy. He didn't care a hoot for the traffic jam, the ear-piercing horns of the cars, cycles, rickshaws, and scooters crowding the road. Instead, he clapped and smiled and explained in his own way how much his mother loved him, that their goat had given birth to two new kids, that he went to the weekly *haat* to sell aubergines, raw papaya and banana flowers. So many things to talk about! Both of them were absorbed with each other's peculiar way of communicating.

On returning home, they parted ways near Prasen's

house. Dunoi lived in the room attached to Prasen's house but the new boy stayed with other employees in the dormitory behind the motor-parts shop. At night, as he tossed and turned on his bed, Dunoi thought about his day and planned to meet his friend again to talk, to share the many things still left unsaid.

The next day the puja was performed at the garage. Dunoi could not see his new friend till the sweets and fruits offered to the god was distributed. He checked from time to time as he went about his chores. Lunch was being cooked for all – *khichdi* with rice and pulses and *labda*, a mixed vegetable curry. The air was filled with the enticing smell of the food. Other workers employed by Prasen also arrived. They sat with a few guests inside the room to have lunch.

'Who's there in the shop?' Prasen asked.

'Sir, that new boy is there,' they replied.

'Okay, send him here for lunch once you go back,' Prasen said.

Dunoi heard them. So they had left him alone there. But he would not have lunch without his friend, he decided. The new boy did not have anyone else in this place; he had arrived only yesterday. He decided he would carry his lunch too and they could eat together. He took *khichdi* and *labda*, enough for two, on a paper plate. He left through the opening in the temporary tent put up in the plot and arrived at the road crossing. The road was deserted today. Dunoi looked to the left. A car was coming. Dunoi let it pass. The hot *khichdi* was burning his palms. He tried to cross the road. There was another car coming from the right side. He did not see it.

Like the khichdi flung on the road, uneaten, Dunoi's hope of making a friend remained unfulfilled.

Even Tagore Said So

Anamika Borah

Little Puchipuchi with soft, white fur, often seen peeing at the gates of the houses, started barking when he saw the black and white Mijuprova. Miju halted at the gate, scared. Puchipuchi hung onto the grill of the veranda with his paws and barked even more ferociously, as if he would bite Miju. She would have loved to touch the soft fur of the little dog and so took no offence at his aggressive tone. Still a bit afraid, Miju climbed the steps to the veranda. She found the calling bell next to the gate. She hesitated. Should she, shouldn't she? Then she jabbed at the bell anyway. A young girl opened the door who, upon seeing Miju, hid behind the curtain and peeped at her. Then she ran inside. Probably she was a

---

Original Title: Rabindranathao kole…

maid in the house of Soladhora 'Sir'. Miju could hear her telling someone – perhaps sir's wife – 'O Baideu, come and see, an odd-looking woman is at the gate. She is all black and white!'

Miju was not surprised. The girl was scared by the black and white patches on her face and hands. Miju braced herself to face another pair of eyes that would burn into her. She was right. A new pair of eyes stared at her now. Miju tried her best to put forward the image of a smart, lively woman to impress the lady. Smiling sweetly, she asked, 'Is this the house of Arup Soladhora Sir?'

'Yes.'

The woman did not say anything more, so she invited herself in, saying, 'If you don't mind, may I sit down inside?'

The woman's eyes were questioning.

'I mean, in the veranda?'

'Yes. Please come in.'

Miju was about to go towards the veranda when the dog barked. She ran back to the gate and cried out to the lady, 'Baideu! Please hold the dog!'

'Jimi, stop! Stop it! Oh, he has become very bad-mannered these days, I don't know why. Jimi, stop! Stop, Jimi!'

Jimi listened to the command barked out in a stylish tone. He hung out his tongue, smelled the stranger and stopped barking. Miju sat down on a chair in the veranda.

'What's it about?' the woman asked without any warmth in her voice, holding onto the dog's chain. 'Why do you want to speak with him?'

'Sir wanted to buy an insurance policy. He had asked me to come today. His tax slab has increased.'

'How do you know?'

Miju could assess the woman's thoughts. She knew how to manage such women. If she could exalt the husband's position, she would be more receptive.

'Not only I, everybody knows,' Miju said. 'All the high officials face high tax problems.'

That to be taxed could be something to be proud of she learnt from Mukta. Everybody knew that Mukta had come into the tax category. She had asked Mukta, what it means to be taxed.

'You won't understand, Miju! The salary is increasing, you know,' Mukta had said.

'Oh?'

'But the increase has only created problems for us.'

'Why?'

'Now we have to pay tax.'

'He is in the tax net, and I didn't know!' The woman seemed agitated by the information. She went inside the house, muttering to herself, 'Oh, what a bore he is, doing all these foolish things. Ajan is already there. Why does he have to purchase policies from anyone else?'

Miju was used to this kind of welcome. By now, she

was thick-skinned enough not to be affected and refused to be flustered. Like a tortoise hiding its face under its crust, she ignored the insult. Arup Soladhora was not a bad man. He was a DRDA officer and quite well off too. He contributed to the funds not only for building the Shiva temple, but also for the Durga Puja celebrations in the locality.

Miju had actually approached him in the office. Bhimananda, a Fourth Grade employee in the office, had introduced her to him. Bhima said that he would help her to sell policies to the staff in the office in lieu of a commission.

'What were you doing all this time,' Bhima regretfully asked Miju, as he ground the dry tobacco leaves in his palm. 'So many agents have come and managed to convince people to buy policies. And you are coming now? Anyway, now that you have, approach our Sir!'

Miju waited uncertainly, but Bhima winked as he put the lump of tobacco in his mouth and led her to the door of Sir's room, instructing, 'Go, tell him! Speak nicely. If you impress him and he feels kindly, he won't mind helping you.'

Soladhora had already shooed off quite a few agents expressing his unwillingness to buy an insurance policy. But looking at her face, all black and white, he relented and said, 'Ok, come to my house. I have to do something about this tax problem, anyway.'

'When shall I come, Sir?'

'Well, you can come before 12 o' clock.'

'Where is your house, sir?'

The man frowned and pressed the bell on the table to call the Fourth Grade employee. He pointed to Miju and asked him to explain her the location of his house.

Only then Miju realised that one doesn't ask an officer the location of his house.

Something else she had learnt, recently, was that if you call an important person over the phone, you are not supposed to hang up first with a 'So long, sir.' He is the privileged one who decides to hang up, not you. If you do so, his ego is hurt.

Arup Soladhora came out to meet her. He drew aside the curtain of the drawing room and looking at her said, "Why are you sitting in the veranda? Come inside."

Miju felt flustered at this unexpected kind gesture and replied, 'It's all right, Sir! I am fine.'

'No, no, please come inside.'

Miju felt a bit uncomfortable. She did not want to sit like a guest in the drawing room of any client. For her work, a veranda was fine. But she could not refuse the welcoming tone of the man and picking up the plastic file, she entered the living room. He sat on the sofa near her. She moved a little further from him.

Miju started explaining to Soladhora, 'Sir, if you buy a policy of 2.5 lakh, you will have to pay Rs 23,740 yearly.

This is actually an exclusive plan for high earners. It's called Jeevan Sree, a very good policy. Please look at page 180 of our Wings Ready Reckoner and its description. Page 40...'

Soladhora fiddled with the nail of his left-hand thumb and asked,

'How much will be my profit if I pay this yearly amount?'

Profit? What amount? Miju felt trapped. She first thought, should I say around Rs 50 lakh in five years? She had heard that if one wanted to climb the ladder of success, one should be able to convince the other person even if it was a lie, but of course, without getting caught. Frankly, Miju could not calculate fast enough the numerous numbers and charts in the Ready Reckoner. She turned to another page and said, 'If you want to have good profit, you can think of the Jeevan Anand scheme. Please see, it's written here: Jeevan Anand: S.A.+Bonus at the end of PPT risk cover continues for lifetime. It means, Sir, lifetime profit.'

'How much premium will I have to pay?'

Miju scanned Page 170. How many lakhs should I target, she wondered. Three? Or five? Or should I quote 10 lakhs, she wondered. Okay, 10 lakhs would be fine. These are people with money.

'Sir, if you opt for a Rs 10 lakh policy, you will have to pay Rs 2,57,618 yearly.'

'For how many years?'

'Five, for five years.'

'How much will be Rs 2,57,618 times 5?'

Miju opened her eyes wide. Soladhora made the matter easier for her and said,

'In five years Rs 2,57,618 yearly payment will amount to about Rs 13 lakhs."

'Yes, yes, Sir, you're right. It means that after five years instead of Rs 10 lakhs you'd be getting around Rs 20 lakhs.' (*Golmaal hai bhai shob golmaal hai*: Everything is confusing, my friend, very confusing). The lines of the popular Hindi film song buzzed in her head.

'Phoosh!' Soladhora exhaled loudly and looked at the Ready Reckoner. The leaves of the brochure fluttered in the air. He saw the writing: 'If you want happiness for a lifetime, help somebody.'

Miju felt her heart beating faster. Had the man caught her bluff? You are dead, Miju, you are dead. Soladhora read another sentence on the next page, 'If you judge people, you will have no time to love them.'

"Aren't you making a mistake with your calculation?" Soladhora looked at her quizzically.

Miju felt her mouth go dry, like a piece of wood. Have patience, Miju, have patience, she told herself. If you impress this man somehow, you will make more profit in a year than you have been making so far in two years. You will make it, you will and your license won't be cancelled like the last two times.

Yes, it had happened twice. Since she couldn't submit the policies on the due date at the end of the year two years in a row, her licence was withdrawn. She was unable to make an impression on anyone, no one was attracted to her, she failed to conclude a deal. Nobody seemed to love her or took pity on her. Despite that, she could not beg; she was too mortified to do that. But now she must impress this man. But how?

'A smile is a curve that sets things straight.' No, she could not risk a smile. So many of her teeth needed filling.

Miju said with extreme politeness (to get the job done, one must grovel), 'Please Sir! Please, buy a policy for m..m…' The words got stuck in her throat. She wanted to say 'for my sake'. She wanted to say, appealingly, 'Sir, look at me, this helpless, lonely young woman who has been battered by life. For my sake, please buy a policy.' But she couldn't go beyond 'm' for 'my'. She adopted another approach. 'Please buy a policy, sir! You'll get tax benefit. We can only help to ensure the policy but don't get any profit. You are the one who will gain. I am not quoting a high amount. You don't have to go for a high net worth range if you don't want to. If the amount seems too high you can opt for the Jeevan Shree policy meant for common people.'

Soladhora got up from the sofa and said, 'Baideu, it's better that you go to high net worth people. We are common people. We somehow manage to cope with our salary. It's not possible, madam, please go.'

Miju felt the ground slipping away from under her feet. She babbled, 'Sir, sir... I didn't mean to...'

But by then Soladhora had left the room. Miju collected the diary which she had opened to explain the policy terms to Soladhora, the ready reckoner, etc. and put them in the polythene bag. She could hear Soladhora's wife rebuking him as she slammed the door shut, 'When you already have Ajan to do these things why do you call home these unknown people to buy a policy?'

She heard Soladhora reply, 'The woman came to my office, so I thought let me help her and open a policy with her. Now she wants to teach me about "rank".'

Miju felt like banging her head on the wall. Somehow, she had said all the wrong things. She wanted to say something but said something else. Somehow these things always happened to her. Always! If she could not submit the premium on time she would again lose her licence.

No, no, she couldn't let it happen. If she lost her licence, the commission would be held up. How would she cope then? With her commission, she managed the extra expenses in the household. She looked longingly towards the door. Perhaps he would come out? But instead, the maid came out dragging the dog. He started barking as soon as he saw her. Miju shrank in fear and begged the young girl, 'Bhonti, please take him away from here!'

'Jimi, estop, estop!' The girl could not pronounce 'stop' properly. She picked up Jimi. Miju decided to leave.

Outside, the sun was blazing. She suddenly felt very thirsty. She had planned to ask for a glass of water at Soladhora's place. She had left home very early, at 7 o'clock.

She had missed her first target and scolded herself. From now on, be careful about what you say. You must speak sweetly and softly to get the job done. Why do you make this mistake again and again? I feel sorry for you, Miju!

She replied to herself, 'Somehow it happens. I don't do it intentionally. I can't keep track of my words. It just runs helter-skelter when I want to say something proper. I don't understand why my tongue doesn't roll out sweet words. Practise, Miju, practise! Don't you know, practice makes perfect?'

Miju walked to the main road. She had to go to Bidyapur but for that she would have to take a Tempo van. She waited under the peepul tree for a Tempo. Though it was the main road, there was hardly anyone around. The air was fresh and lovely. The flowering Sonaru trees on both sides of the road formed a yellow canopy. She remembered a few lines by her favourite poet Anamika:

Why are you giggling, bathed thus in colour?
I have to ask you
O sonaru...

It was not important what she wrote. Miju had seen her. She was attractive in a placid way. Ah, God sometimes bestows everything on somebody – beauty, brains, etc.

Miju sat down beneath the tree. The Magic buses passed in quick succession. Sometimes a Superbus or a truck went by too. She mourned again the loss of the chance to sell a policy. Why did it happen? Why, oh why, did she make such mistakes?

The colours of life...

Miju wanted to write a few sentences on the now-useless form but a crow cawed from nearby to remind her – Miju, those lyrics are for people who lead a normal life, those who have families. They do not belong to you.

Miju folded the paper. She saw two women on wheelchairs being pushed by two persons across the road. She observed the scene with great interest. She took out her Nokia cell phone and took their picture as they moved. She would show the picture to Simanta. He had been writing a series of stories on these helpless people in his newspaper. If he could write about the women, poor and dressed in old, torn clothes, perhaps they would get some help.

Ouch! An ant bit her toe. She wanted to destroy the little tormentor with her palm but it seemed to say, 'Miju, if you can cry at others' misery, you would be able to get consolation in those tears. If you worry about others, they will worry about you too. Best of luck! You will have success with the next client.'

All is well. All is well. Miju is good. Miju is good. Miju is a very good girl. She tried to give her morale a boost.

Miju took a long breath. Once she arrived at Mukul Khaklari's house in Bidyapur, she must manage to get the policy of Namita Medhi done. From there, through the Panikhowa Road she had to go Bishnupur. 'Miju, don't miss a chance again. You have missed a lot in life. Not anymore. If someone tries to flirt a little, so what? Haven't you seen how people are doing quite well by indulging in the advances made by Bhogeswar Chaleng? And you? You got a chance but didn't take it. Instead you said curtly that after 8 o'clock at night you did not encourage anyone to talk business. Had you indulged him a bit, you wouldn't have had to go around begging people to invest in an insurance policy. Big officers would have listened to your request. Anyway, what is done is done. Now don't miss the next chance.'

O God, my friend in need, if I make a mistake please correct me. I am an innocent girl, I don't know many things, please help me.

Forget it Miju, at least you have remained untouched by worldly wiles even at this age.

As she was waiting for a Tempo, Miju suddenly remembered the discussions about buying a teak log to make furniture for Aimoni's wedding. Jan had asked her for some monetary help, not much, around Rs 5,000. She had dithered at the amount but promised to buy instead clothes for the trousseau, trunk, etc. Jan had agreed.

So today she had to place the order for the trunk and buy the clothes too.

Miju got up suddenly. Aimoni, Aimoni, treasure of my heart, to you I can even give my breath. I have not been able to look you fully in the face since the day the wedding was fixed. You are such a good girl, Aimoni. One cannot find a girl like you these days. You would agree to marry anyone we arrange for you; you've looked after the house so well for so long, you've looked after our mother. My heart breaks at this separation. Even today I left behind the soiled clothes in the bathroom. You won't allow me to touch the rough washing soap, worrying that it would make my fingers become whiter and more painful.

My little sister, the youngest among us. You were born in the year when I was appearing for my matriculation exam. You touched my feet, exploring my toes. Like a soft, white rabbit, you crawled up to my study table. You stood on your toes to reach my knee and called me 'ab-ba', unable to pronounce 'baideu'.

Miju got into a Tempo packed with people. They protested, 'Baideu, how can you go like this? What if you fall down on the road?' But Miju pushed in. Sometimes people had to be shameless. If she became sentimental now and got down from the van, she was the one who was going to suffer. She ignored the insults. She had to reach Bidyapur.

After Aimoni's wedding, her uncle Konkhura's daughter Nilamoni was going to be married. The groom was an engineer in Saudi Arabia. He had proposed while he was a first year B. Sc student. Konkhura was the headmaster of a school. They were not on talking terms, mainly because Miju did not want to. If her uncle saw her in the bazaar or somewhere else, he looked at her as if surprised and said to the person next to him, 'She's my elder brother's daughter.'

Miju's father Dodo died when she was only twenty-one. He died because he used to drink excessively. The brothers fought over this. Her father had lost his job because he had gone to the office drunk and argued with the officer which eventually led to a physical attack. Failing to maintain the family with four children, he drank even more and passed away when he was only 42.

If anyone asked Miju, 'What do you miss most?' she would say, 'My father, Dodo.'

Miju at 21. If she stood against a green backdrop she looked like the soft leaves of a pink flower. She had started to look for a job, but without any success. In her place, the local MLA had given the job to Jan. It was a secure job as a gazetted officer, though sometimes, the salary did not come on time.

At an age when girls fall in love, she had taken over

the responsibility of her siblings. Love, lover, girlfriend were words to be kept at bay. It was not that she didn't like anybody, but her home came before her girlish sentiments. Many a time she lied to those interested in her saying that she was already engaged to someone else.

These days she did not even think of these frivolous things. Nilamoni often said, 'Dangar ba, my dear elder sister, had you been involved in affairs from time to time, then you would not have this horrendous personality. All this roughness, bad manners, stupidity would have vanished. You would have been a sophisticated lady.'

'How so, my dear?'

'It's simple. If a boy had touched you, at least, you would not have abused him instantly, calling him a cur.'

'Oh, leave it! I feel shy to talk about these things. Do you think an old Salika bird could learn to speak? How many days are left for me to live anyway?'

'You can fall in love at any age, Dangar- ba. You just need the capacity to feel. You don't have that capacity. It's zero.'

Miju knew why Nilamoni always emphasised the word 'capacity.' Miju slipped away at such moments. Nothing, but nothing, seemed attractive to her these days. She could only feel a sadness engulfing her at all times. When she returned home, after chasing people for insurance policies the whole day and then went to her room after freshening up, she would feel as if she were sinking into a whirlpool of seawater. Nobody around her knew about the tears she shed in her lonesome moments.

For the last few months Miju had been feeling like a field which had remained under water throughout the year.

There was no particular reason why she should suddenly feel so mournful. As the days passed, new grief added to her misery.

Like today. A new sorrow has been added to her bag of misery, melancholy at her own ineptitude, at the failure to use the right word at the right moment.

Mukul Khakhlari of Bidyapur agreed to buy a policy of small amount with a half-yearly premium of Rs 1,754. He said his brother-in-law was also an agent who had made him take a policy that was worth a big amount. Mrs Khakhlari insisted on making a cup of tea for her. Then she looked at her hands and face and suggested, 'Baideu, you can consult a good skin doctor for your problem. Oh, I really feel bad. You are such a pretty girl.'

Miju felt as if the tea would spurt out of her mouth. Was this woman joking? She told Miju about a good doctor whose clinic was on Rajgarh Road. Miju kept quiet. After all, she couldn't tell Mrs Khakhlari that she no longer regretted that her once-fair face was now a collage of black and white patches. I am not anyone's girlfriend, Mrs Khakhlari, it doesn't matter; I don't have to have a face that a lover would like to kiss.

Suddenly, Miju wanted to hug Mrs Khakhlari tight and howl, like the little girl she once was when she was often called a crybaby.

Surprisingly, this desire to cry loudly often came over Miju these days, as if it was her only dream, her only wish. If only she had somebody to relate to, whose sympathy could move her to cry her heart out. She did not like anything these days. But if she happened to like somebody suddenly, what will happen?

From Mrs Khakhlari's house she entered Namita Medhi's house. Namita Medhi chatted endlessly. Miju looked at her cell phone. Twenty minutes past 11 am. Namita Medhi said she would buy only a policy for a payment of Rs 325 a month. Miju was disappointed. She had hoped that Namita Medhi would buy a more lucrative policy. For this puny amount she had been patiently listening to Namita Medhi's incessant *bakwas baat* (nonsense). However, she helpfully suggested to Miju to check out the house on the opposite side belonging to Uttama Chowdhury.

'But is she there? The door is shut...'

'Yes. She has returned from college a little while ago and I saw her going to the terrace in her skimpy dress,' Namita Medhi said.

Not only a college teacher, but wearing a skimpy three-quarter dress! Miju could feel her chest jumping with apprehension. But she shook it off and knocked on the door. Uttama Chowdhury opened the door looking like a teenager.

Miju joined her hands respectfully and greeted, 'Namaskar!'

'Yes, tell me.'

Miju felt a little flustered but said, 'I have come from the LIC office…'

'Sorry baideu! Actually I don't know these things. My mister is an extension officer. He...'

If she could speak with such accent and style to Miju, God only knows how she spoke to young guys. Like a river eagerly meeting the sea?

Miju left. On the way she would go to the bazaar to place the order for the trunk and buy the clothes. She did not have to buy all on the same day. After that, if she had time, she would go to Runjun's place and have something to eat.

But before that she had a most important visit to finish. Now it was ten past twelve. Field Officer Debarshi Sir did not come to office before 1 o' clock. She must meet Debarshi Gautam. She had heard that they were going to open an LIC outlet to cover the whole area. The inauguration was to happen in a couple of days.

Since he was an officer from Assam, many agents like Miju had been requesting a post in the new office. Debarshi was the only Assamese officer in the branch. He had spoken sternly when Miju had lost the licence twice. But it was an impartial way of scolding. Miju wondered if he even noticed the black and white patches on her face like others did. She never saw any surprise or pity in his face when he looked at her. Most agents had left unable to reach the target. Miju could not do that. Her life depended on it. It was the only thing that kept her busy, ensured some earnings and now her only love. She would have to stay even if Debarshi gave her a dressing down. At the meetings Debarshi would say, 'Why can't you manage to obtain 12 policies? Do you know my performance record is the worst in the circle? I can't compete because of agents like you. In the past if an annual target of 12 policies could be reached it was fine, but not anymore. The target is Rs 1 lakh now.'

Earlier, Miju and the other agents had got together to somehow rustle up the mandatory 12 policies though somebody would take a policy at only Rs 280 premium, somebody else perhaps Rs 120. But these days it was not possible. What would they do now? Especially as there was an LIC agent in every house. Professors, schoolteachers, all and sundry, opened agencies in the name of their wives and managed to grab the clients. People wanted to earn money with both hands.

Miju had been working with Debarshi for seven years. She had never seen an Assamese fellow work at such pace. He did not waste a single minute. He did his field duty with devotion. At times, out in the field she would bump into him. On these occasions he would nod at her in recognition. He was strict with the agents but not discourteous. He used harsh words when necessary and could be absolutely unforgiving sometimes. One day, facing his fury during a meeting Aparna had burst into tears. Her phone rang a few times during the meeting. Debarshi switched off the speaker and ordered, 'Out, out! I am saying, you go out of the room. Are you the only young woman here? What could be so important that you get calls again and again? Tell him you are in a meeting. Otherwise get out of the room.'

Aparna cried as she clarified, 'The call was from home. They wanted to know if I had taken the key to the suitcase.'

Debarshi did not spare anyone.

Now Miju saw that her colleagues Aparna, Tanaya, Pratiksha, Debanga and Arijit were already there, waiting to meet Debarshi. They smiled at her. Aparna gave up her chair for Miju.

'''How are you, Miju-ba?' she asked.

'Pulling on somehow,' she replied. 'What about you?'

'Oh, first class.'

'If everything is fine, why are you walking around in the sun chasing LIC policies? You should have relaxed in a coffee house,' Miju said.

'Oh, came to see my man. Without seeing him I feel sad, you know!'

Aparna talked like that. She had absorbed the scolding in the meeting and now referred to Debarshi as her husband. Pratiksha and Tanaya were equally naughty and said, 'Ok, done. You take the upper portion, we will take the lower portion.'

Miju loved these girls. They could make light of the most vexing situations in life. Young people, old people, they didn't care. They said whatever they wanted to say.

Aparna held a special corner in her heart. If only she could bring her home as her brother Jan's wife. If she could, she would have told the lovely bride, 'You won't face any problem with me. Not even an iota. This white colour of my skin is not contagious, it doesn't spread to others. Actually it happens due to a bad liver. And you know, if the purple light of the sun that filters through the holes in the ozone layer in the atmosphere reaches somebody's skin...'

She tried to remember when she first faced the odd situation. Oh yes, the day when her cousin Majoni, Apa aunty's daughter, was getting married and she was serving sweets. She was trying to find a spoon but not finding it, she picked up a sweet with her two fingers. The woman she was serving looked at her fingers and uttered '*ish*!' and then stopped.

For a long time now Miju had stopped going to any relative's place. She didn't attend any wedding either. She was afraid of standing naked under the scrutinising eyes and gossip about her suffering from 'white leprosy'. Miju hated the pitying glances and so called sympathetic words. Of course, she felt sorry for herself. Shouldn't she? It was natural. At first, there were flecks of white on her skin like grains of rice powder. Those slowly spread across her skin, turning them black. And that pretty, bright girl saw her skin covered with white patches, like the leaves of the jasmine flower. As if a full moon had broken into pieces and covered different portions of her body. Tell me, if such injustice was done who wouldn't feel devastated?

At first, Miju stealthily touched her face and fingers many times. The white patches had increasingly made her feel lonely, depressed and uneasy in front of others. Slowly she withdrew within herself . Her younger uncle's daughter Runjun's five-year-old daughter Dhunusha touched her fingers and asked her in baby-talk language, 'Mi, have you burnt your fingers?'

On her part, Runjun, taking care to be sensitive to her feelings, would advise, 'Mi, don't eat things like eggs. Not only for the skin, but for your own good.'

These days she often said, 'It's becoming quite common, you know, this skin problem. You at least are grown up. You know, Haren-da's daughter is developing this too and she's only in Class Three. People suffer from so many serious diseases. In comparison, yours is nothing.'

Yes, Miju knew that too. It was not a serious disease but it made a harsh impact on one's psychology. The mind feels empty. It makes you want to hide behind a leaf, want to submerge under the sea and makes you want to become invisible to inquisitive eyes. Oh, those looks, like sharp daggers. They seemed to say, 'Your skin is slowly becoming a playfield of darkness and light, it's like a landscape drawn in black and white.'

But it did not make Miju into a statue frozen in wretchedness. Her family looked after her with great care and love. Aimoni, Sonjoni, Runjun, all surrounded her with love. Moon, friend of her brother Jan, would try to catch her palms and say, 'Dangar-ba, is this a disease? Really, you are...'

Miju smiled as she thought of Moon. One day he had brought his guitar to play jazz music for her and sang, 'There's a very naughty girl, Dangar-ba. She's like you. I love her so much, but she doesn't, do you know? I am suffering, it's a tragedy.'

He often tried to make her laugh.

When Miju was young she often lost herself in odd thoughts. She imagined how she would suffer from a serious illness and people would visit her, bringing packets of biscuits and sweets. They would speak fondly. Some would give her money. With that money she would have mutton curry to her heart's content.

Her mother used to tell her guests visiting their home, 'She had a perfect complexion. There was not a stain in her face, not even a black spot. She used to wear a pink frock. With that frock...'

'Why don't you perform *charak* puja? And sun bath?' some advised her mother.

'Will you do it, my dear?' Her mother had asked Miju.

'What, Ma?'

'They say you have to immerse your body in the water and keep looking at the sun.'

Miju did not have the heart to tell her mother who never believed in rituals, and now felt so helpless that she was begging for blessings from the Sun God.

'This is not a disease, Ma. This happens to many people. You know, a girl in Class Three living in the house next door to Runjun also has a similar condition.'

Her mother felt reassured. If so many people had this problem then her daughter had others to share the suffering. Still, if only her daughter's face had escaped the scourge. As a girl, her face was important. A pretty face always melted hearts. No, her face was not spared – her nose, eyes, eyebrows, were all shadowed by the affliction.

Debarshi was in his room. Miju, Pratiksha, Aparna – all the other agents wanted the post of office assistant. All of them had a diploma in computers too. There were four posts. Of them two would be direct recruits from the head office. So Debarshi had two posts to fill. Whom would he choose? Mijuprova sat outside Debashri's glass-walled room. When there were women like Aparna and

Patiksha she could not expect to be chosen. Even though there were two posts, it was most likely that only one would be appointed and he or she would have to work overtime. All companies did the same thing. So she took it for granted that she would miss the bus. Moreover, there was her dismal record of missing targets. She had just about managed to deliver.

Miju got ready to leave. She felt depressed. Among the agents, her performance was the worst. She was not competent on the computer either. When she got up to go, she looked back and saw Upanga Kalita gesturing her to come in.

Miju entered the room and stood behind Aparna. Debarshi shocked everybody present by asking her, 'Can you learn how to operate the computer within three months and manage the work here?'

Was the field officer addressing her?, Miju wondered. But when she saw all the others looking at her, she became sure. Yes, he was addressing her!

'Yes, I can,' Miju replied promptly.

Yes, she could. Why not? Give me another chance... Suddenly Miju sang to herself:

Give me some sunshine

Give me some rain

Give me another chance...

'Ok. I'll give you another chance,' Debashri said. He pointed his finger as if it was a baton and said, 'But remember, we want performance.'

'Yes, Sir!' Miju's despair vanished and she answered like a soldier to her commander.

Aparna and the others smiled. Good, they were not jealous of her. The next day the new office would be inaugurated. Miju's work would also start then. Her friends made her give them a treat.

Miju finished her job of ordering a trunk for Aimoni's wedding and a few clothes. She was happy enough to avoid dropping at Runjun's place for some grub and spent Rs 10 on two plates of savoury crunchy *phuchka* balls.

She reached home in an elated mood. Truly, she had spent a very fruitful day today. She had a bath, had dinner and went to her room. She felt extremely grateful to Debarshi. A certain attraction stirred in her heart. Debarshi was so good. He had treated a woman like her with such kindness. She hummed the lines from Rabindranath's poem:

Jibon jakhan shukaye jai
Karuna dharay egou
Sokol madhuri lukaye jai
Geet sudha-rase esho
(When the essence of life dries up
Come as the flow of compassion
When all the pleasantness hides away
Come as the nectar of melody)

Suddenly Miju remembered Aparna's face. Somehow she felt now that Aparna had not been that open with her. She had noticed both Pratiksha and Aaprna looking at each other in a particular way.

Miju was slipping into a light sleep. The phone came alive with the ping of an incoming message. She opened the message box ...970...the message was from Debarshi Sir. No, it couldn't be an official message. She felt her heart run faster; her hands trembled.

'Dear agent, I'm sorry to say that U r cancelled for the post of ...s your performance is poor.'

After she left the office, was there a reappraisal on the basis of performance? Miju didn't want to know. She knew that every girl on earth, every woman, was better than her in performance.

She would be working in the new office in town, she had SMSed her close associates like Runjun, Moon and others. Runjun had called and instructed how she should dress, how she should conduct herself on the first day in the office. Despite a very busy schedule Moon had congratulated her and said his usual dialogue, 'I am in a tragic situation. When will people understand my state of affairs?'

Now what was she going to tell them? How could she take back the words already spoken? And erase the hopes raised? People like Debarshi Gautam were so mechanical, so unattached. How could a handsome face destroy conscience and wisdom at one stroke? Or perhaps he was helpless? Miju tried to reason. Perhaps one day she would know the real reason the two nominees from the head office refused to work along with her. After all, there was the matter of public interest. Even she herself could regret the decision, right?

Miju was now like a submerged field in monsoon. Once again she sank in the overflowing water. Moon was calling. She was annoyed, what a time to call to crack jokes. When he saw that she didn't pick up the phone, he sent a message: "Mi, do you know what Rabindranath said? *maan dibo je temon maani noitu ami..*

Miju shook herself out of the stupor. She held onto every word the poet wrote - *maan dibo je temon maani noitu ami.*

(I am not dignified enough
to bestow dignity upon you)

The phone pinged again

'You too never gave me *maan*, Mi! Oh leave, don't talk to me. I have divorced you, final.'

Moon's jokes failed to comfort Miju today. She got swept away with the words of Rabindranath: *maan dibo je temon maani noitu ami...*

Flight to Freedom

Geetali Borah

And one day, the bird flew away from his grasp with a flutter. Perhaps after a long flight, tired, she has now chosen to rest in a landscape of burnt timber and sharp black stones where she is singing a sweet melody full of hope, her wings colouring the barren land, which would probably soon turn green and soothing...

He felt an emptiness creeping deep into his heart.

Sleep eluded him.

His eyes turned dry, his lips had forgotten how to break into a smile.

Please give me back the bird, he prayed silently, his mind straying even as he sat face to face with Sunanda. She smothered his parched lips with her bee-stung lips

---

Original Title: Uron

smeared with orange lipstick. She said coquettishly, 'Whom are you thinking of now? Why don't you look at me?' He tried to smile. She looked alluring, dressed in a grey T-shirt with a plunging neckline and an off-white pair of jeans. Absent mindedly, he ran his hand over her body but inwardly he was panicking. Was his hand seeking something in an empty space?

He turned his back to her, feeling equally drained.

His mother was diagnosed with cancer of the uterus. The quiet woman who stoically bore her pain had left it festering for too long and now the crab had eaten into her guts. They knew she was not going to live much longer. Every evening when he returned home, he could hear the moans from her room.

His father, as usual, was preoccupied with his music and a glass of imported liquor. The lyrical notes from a bamboo flute and the tinkling sound of glasses reached him. Was it Tibetan or a Chinese folk song, he would wonder.

From his sister's room came the sound of a TV programme. Even then, from time to time, he could hear guarded conversation with someone on the mobile phone, accompanied with flirtatious giggles.

As usual, this evening too, he stood in the doorway and asked, 'How are you today, Ma?'

A putrid odour that the clinical smell of medicines and the scent from lighted joss-sticks could not smother, assailed his nose. He brought out a hanky from his pocket and covered his nose.

His mother tried to smile. A cynical smile hovered over her face, ravaged with pain. 'I am fine,' she replied.

He felt as if the talons of the vicious crabs that had eaten away at his mother's innards were now crawling towards him. He ran away from there. He tried to hide in the safety of his room but discovered that he felt nothing, absolutely nothing. The bird had really flown away – when did that happen? Leaving him alone, distraught.

He searched desperately for the bird. He felt uncertain, wondering how he would go through life without the melody of its song and the rhythmic sound of its colourful flapping wings.

He felt tired, very tired.

To get away from the fruitless search he had reached out to Esther. She taught chemistry in one of the leading colleges in the city. Esther Kikon was like a wind from the hills – strong, and untamed. She led him into a heaven of forbidden pleasures, introduced him to pure ecstasy.

In her well-decorated drawing room, the smoke from her cigarette drew abstract patterns in the air.

'Have you heard from Manasi?' she asked.

He looked at her as if he could not comprehend the question. Then nonchalantly, as if brushing away a speck of dust from his shirt, he replied, 'Oh, she has sent the divorce papers.'

Esther laughed hysterically. She didn't seem able to stop. She sounded like the gurgling water of a restless stream from the hills. Her husband lived in Delhi. Her small, sharp eyes danced as she said, 'Goldie shows me the nude picture of the call girl he invites into his bed. I am sure he also doesn't expect that in his absence I am pining and playing on the strings of a *tanpura*.'

The evening got more intimate. Esther's bedroom was awash in a soft blue light. Her slim body quivered as if touched by a breeze from the hills. It seemed to transport him to another plane. Desperately he searched for his lost bird in her body warm with desire, in her soft lips and in the eyes now closed waiting expectantly for the climax of union.

But he did not find the bird.

Not even a blade of green grass escaped from the red beak of the bird to offer him solace.

His body, on the verge of reaching the peak, shrank abruptly. A deep tiredness and helplessness invaded him. His manhood turned slack and lay like the wrinkled, abandoned old skin of a snake.

Like one possessed, he often searched for the bird in the lanes and by-lanes of the city. Standing beside the mighty Brahmaputra, he lifted his arms in a welcoming gesture and called out, 'Please come to me, O my bird – come, please, please!'

Standing beneath an ancient tree and looking at the

ball of the red sun slowly sinking into the water, he called again and again, '*Pokhi,* my little bird, come, come to me!'

His heart-rending cry travelled aimlessly in the emptiness and then bounced back to him.

As if by routine, today too, he stopped at the door to his mother's room and asked, 'Ma, how are you today?'

The woman, smelling of rotting flesh, medicine and lighted joss sticks, had a fixed ironic smile on her lips.

'Fine, I am fine,' she replied.

He passed by his father's room on the way to his room. As usual, the sound of tinkling glass and recorded music wafted out from the room. From his sister's room came the sound of conversation in a hushed voice and the echo of conspiratorial laughter.

The green plant Manasi had carefully nurtured in the flower pot had now dried up. The clothes-horse and Godrej almirah were in shambles. The bedsheet had not been washed for a long time. Everything seemed to be in a state of flux. From the drawer he brought out the divorce papers Manasi had sent for his signature. He signed it. He would hand it over to her the next day.

Aimlessly he searched, behind the statue of the Laughing Buddha, Manasi's dressing table, under the cushion on the sofa that stood to one side of the bedroom. Suppose the bird had left behind a few tufts of feather from its golden wings? Or even a strand. Ah, if he could find some remnant of that bird!

Manasi had not liked the bird. 'One day it will take you away from me with false promises and cunningness,' she had said.

'Whoa! This little bird surely can't intrude into our relationship that is glued together with Fevicol,' he had said with a laugh. 'Remember you loved it too when it took me to you flying over the blue forest. You had said, on its wings you could soar above the earth and feel something ethereal, out of this world.'

'You are right. But your bird is so restless; it doesn't want to settle down. This home I have built with love and dreams, if it doesn't like it, won't it feel empty?' she had said sadly.

And sure enough, perhaps not so much as attempting to find a new resting place, but wanting to explore a new garden, a fresh fragrance or taste a ripe new fruit, his bird flew here and there.

It whispered in his ears, 'Listen, there's only one life. To discover even a bit of this mysterious beautiful world, a lifetime is not enough.'

He had loved the bird, trusted it. In fact, he had become one with it.

That's why he had even flown, like the bird, to far-off Africa.

He had met Jonala in the exciting world of social network. Afterwards, through Skype and video conversations, he met the student of mass communications from a well-known university there. How vivacious she was, intelligent and sensitive! He often marvelled at her.

The mental satisfaction of interacting was followed by emotional nearness and at last, physical intimacy hanging between the real and the virtual world. To reach each other, they concocted their own little ways. From the computer screen Jonala reached out to him with her thick eyebrows, full lips and inviting eyes. He kissed her. Her unusually pointed full breasts held him mesmerised.

Did his bird fly away to Jonala? He switched on the laptop hurriedly and sent a message to her. He received the reply after half an hour.

After another half an hour he readied himself for another kind of flight and shut the door.

Jonala seemed anxious, and sad too, on the laptop screen.

'What's happened to you? I have sent so many mails but no answers. You okay? I am really worried.' Jonala went on speaking in her incorrect English.

'Do you love me?' he asked.

'What kind of question is this? I like being with you, I enjoy chatting with you. You know so many things! And you are so sensitive...'

'Can you show me your boobs?' he asked impatiently.

Jonala observed him for some time. Looking deeply into his eyes she tried to measure his restlessness with her usual sensitivity. Then as if it was quite normal, she bared her breasts from underneath the off-white shirt and red bra. He examined intensely the light and shadow on her breasts displayed on his computer screen.

No, his bird was not hidden between her breasts.

'Come on dear,' Jonala begged him to touch the screen. He did not feel aroused. Rather, the outsized black nipples on her breasts reminded him of a dead *gandhipuk,* the smelly flying bug.

'Sorry, Jonala, I just wanted to see you once,' he said and switched off the laptop.

He lay on the bed. The ceiling was like a sky, from where oppressive chunks of monsoon clouds hung, gloomy and unsure of the future.

His father's mechanical enjoyment of the evening, his mother's moans, his sister's selfishness, left him feeling trapped in a cage.

He somehow felt that for his father, a high-ranking bank official, his mother was something like the foreign liquor he sipped every evening. Or an item in the archive of folk music he had built up meticulously, collected from every corner of the country and abroad. Perhaps he had preferred her in her domesticated role, cooking different varieties of gourmet food in her younger days and when the perfume of her body and its meandering lines he liked to explore in the darkness of the night.

He knew that his mother had a boxful of clothes in

rich colours with matching blouses embroidered with shiny beads. She also had designer sandals to go with them. Perhaps she took pride in these luxuries when she was younger. But his father never allowed her to wear those clothes. He had never seen his mother wear anything else but *mekhela sador* in different shades of white, sometimes perhaps a golden Muga set with motifs in green when she went out with her husband to some official function or a family get-together.

When he was in college, one day he suddenly came across his mother sitting in front of the box with its flap open, tenderly running her fingers through the colourful clothes. He felt as if a sharp thorn had pierced his heart.

After his post-graduation, when he was working with an NGO in Delhi, he had asked his mother to come and stay with him for a few days. His mother refused right away.

'If I go, your father will have a difficult time managing everything,' she said. Who could argue with that logic?

Yet, his father, who roamed the hills and seas of the world in the company of his friends, had never taken her along. Sure he had married a beautiful girl from an aristocratic family but he never regarded her as a fit companion for him. In fact, in some careless moments, he let the sentiment slip through too.

But after his mother became bedridden, one day he saw from the doorstep that his mother was wearing a blouse with shiny embroidery and a red-green sari with a golden border. She was resting against the bedstead, her cheeks pink. Was it rouge she was wearing? And his father was sitting next to her, reading something to her.

He slipped away quietly, unwilling to disturb this tableau of the most beautiful sight in the world.

The next day when he opened the almirah in his bedroom, between the folds of Manasi's pink khadi kurta, he discovered a few golden strands, perhaps left behind long time ago by his elusive bird.

The next day, he went to meet Manasi. He stood waiting, agitated and restless, as she emerged from the common room of the school.

'Tell me.' Manasi looked at him directly, with piercing eyes.

He had planned to say so many things but now they lay scattered on the ground. He sounded incoherent, like a child trying to form his first words.

After a long time, he asked, 'How are you?'

As soon as he uttered the words, he realised that it was a stupid question. Her glowing face, the confident walk and luminous eyes told him that Manasi was doing fine. Nothing seemed to have changed for her. Rather she looked more self-assured.

'How are you?' Manasi asked him.

'I am fine, I am fine,' he replied, talking fast.

He would have liked to tell her about his lost bird. Instead, he stood in front of her like a lost child at a fair.

'Would you like a cup of coffee?' Manasi asked him.

'No, it's fine,' he replied and handed over the papers.

He stood at the doorway of his mother's room and asked mechanically, 'How are you, Ma?'

But he saw that she was sleeping, her head on his father's lap. Her face was serene, a kind of peace he had never seen before. And his father was running his fingers through her hair as if she were a child.

Suddenly from beyond the emptiness, he could hear the sound of the bird singing *ree...ree...ree.* He recognised it at once, the call of his lost bird.

Impatient and excited, he ran out of the room.

Daylight had left but darkness was yet to spread its *aanchal* across the horizon. There was not even a shadow of a single flying bird in the sky. The concrete buildings and a few trees were washed in the soft light of dusk. Perhaps his bird was hiding in this landscape of light and shadow.

He lifted his arms and called out, "O my bird, come! Please come to me!'

His voice bounced off the lifeless concrete walls and echoed.

Come back, come back, O my bird

I won't keep you locked in a golden cage

Don't be afraid — come, come to me!

I will let you sleep cocooned in the crimson web of my heart inside the ribs – come!

I will give you a free sky to fly – to breathe
Come back to my heart
I will feed you sweet grains soaked in my heart's blood
If you want to hurt me with your beak, I will open my heart
Come back to me, my *prem,* my love – come to me!

Mini

Bonti Senchowa

Beginning

It is a pristine morning. The heat of the sun is yet to reach its full intensity. The air is not murky enough to portend an imminent earthquake. Neither is there a gloominess to warn of an upcoming storm. There is no intermittent rain, a precursor to an unseasonal flood. In short, everything is fine, the morning is unsullied. No quarrelsome voices in the background, no shouting. Batches of leech, hidden in the wild plants lining the path leading to the toilet outside the main house, waiting for a victim, are absent too. A colourful bird the size of a mynah jumps down from the Sthalapadma flower tree. It hops here and there looking for insects to fill its hungry

---

Original Title: Mini

stomach and croons softly. She is happy for no particular reason, but happy, nonetheless. The mornings are like this for her now. Clean and pure. She feels she could sing forever like the bird without getting tired. As it pecks at her food, she turns its little neck, the ears, alert trying to catch some sound, perhaps expecting something untoward to happen.

The house wakes up slowly to the daily routine. Stretching itself from the night's slumber, the activities gather pace. The toothbrushes in the mouths seem to pause a little. Still, they have not stopped altogether. The water taps spout open. The voices now become more routine and louder. Mini! Mini! Different voices call out. Without Mini, the household cannot function. She is invaluable in the smooth running of the house.

Mini wakes up. She touches her bed. She had spent the night on this bed. Clean. Soft. This is her second day in this house. How beautiful is the morning! Somebody calls her softly. She makes the bed and goes out of the room. She would have to help out a little in the household chores but her main job is to play with the little baby and keep him occupied. Sure, at first she was a bit apprehensive but curious too. But food, clothes and a shelter – she is getting all this – what else she could ask for?

By now the household is in full swing with varied sounds emanating from here and there. The pressure cooker whistles loudly. From behind the doors of the bathrooms comes the sound of water, like pouring monsoon rain. The irritating sound of the doors of the steel almirah opening comes from some rooms. Somewhere a clothes hangar falls on the floor. Mini is summoned to pick it up. Time to arrange food on the dining table. Mini, Mini! Come here! People from different rooms congregate around the dining table. They attack the food simultaneously, somebody eats standing buffet-style, while others sit down for the meal. A baby's cry announces its arousal. Expectantly, all of them troop to the room to greet the prince. But through the opening in the crowd, the baby only sees Mini. After only one day with her, he opens his eyes wide as if he remembers and looks at her steadily. Then he opens his mouth in a toothless smile and bends towards her as if saying, 'Come, take me in your lap.'

The people in the house are happy. Relieved. Good, the main purpose is served. The baby likes Mini. She listens to the instructions as she continues her chores. After sometime, all of them leave for work. Including the baby's mother. When they leave, Mini goes to shut the main gate. A newspaper from a corner of the veranda rustles. The head of the family keeps it aside and calls her, 'Hey girl! Come here!'

Was he calling her to pluck his grey hairs, she wonders. She had been instructed to station herself near the baby and keep an eye on him. Mini approaches the head of the house hesitantly. She finds him inspecting her from head to toe. His measured glance makes her feel uncomfortable and she looks down at her feet. Her smile disappears. She is not able to lift her eyes.

'Look at me! Let me have a look at you.'

His voice is tender. She puts aside her shyness and fear and straightens up. She looks back at him.

'Have you had your period?'

Mini stands still, shocked. The smile leaves her face. Her ears and face are aflame in embarrassment. She has heard what he said all right, but cannot understand what to make of it. Mini knows answers to many questions. Like, do you know how to iron clothes? Do you know how to use the pressure cooker? Can you pluck grey hairs from an old man's head? But what is this man asking? Isn't it something the mistress of the house is supposed to ask? The question hovers in the silence on the veranda. The questioning, hungry eyes of the man make her uncomfortable. If only she could disappear into the earth, right where she was standing. But her helplessness only seems to encourage the man.

His eyes and the lecherous lips seem like a *khaloi,* a basket full of restless little fish.

'Can't you understand? I am asking you if you have become a big girl, stupid!'

'No, I haven't,' she replies. She is worried. What kind of answer was the *malik* expecting? That she had already attained puberty? Or not yet? If he didn't like her answer, would he drive her away? She shrinks into a huddle in shame, fear and indecision.

'Looking at your figure one would think you've already become a young maiden. You are really very beautiful, you know. But it's not a good thing that you haven't yet attained puberty. It's a bad disease. You won't get a groom.'

Mini stands stock still. Instinctively she understands that something untoward has happened. The air in the veranda is now polluted. Is there an animal hiding behind the green tea bush ready to pounce on her? She is scared. Somewhere, a line had been crossed. Something dirty and sickly pierces through the frock she is wearing and climbs up her thighs. Sheer terror shows in her face, her eyes. Her nostrils flare up in disgust. She tries to smile uncertainly but instead she breaks into tears. She wants to run inside but her feet seem rooted to the floor. She tries to pull her frock down as if to protect herself from something obscene.

'You don't have to worry. I am here for you. Everything will be taken care of. Only don't talk anything about it to others. This is between you and me. Are you feeling shy? Come, come here!'

A hairy hand reaches out to her. Its ugly shadow blackens the innocent aura of the cool morning. The little bird has now abandoned the Sthalapadma tree in search of insects while singing incessantly. But it squeaks in terror seeing a poisonous snake coming towards it from the fork of the tree. Her little heart shakes like a thousand earthquakes. Like in the proverbial story in mythology, the sea dries up for her. The precious stones disappear somewhere. The river changes its course. The hills sink into the earth's bowl and to the surface springs up a thorny tree of betrayal and uncertainty.

The baby starts crying from the room inside. He is not used to being left alone for so long, he is perhaps telling her.

Terrified, Mini goes to the bathroom. It is her allotted bathroom. Shutting the door she can exhale at last. In this small, closed space she feels free. 'Ma, Ma,' she cries out. But who is her mother? The woman who gave birth to her and cut the umbilical cord as proof of her motherhood? The sound ricochets from the closed door. Did she ever have a chance to utter this endearment as she kept moving from house to house as a maid? And who is her father? The man who visits at the end of the month to collect her salary from her employer? That's all the connection she has with her parents.

'Hey girl! Why don't you come out of the bathroom? Who will finish all these chores if you keep yourself in the bathroom for so long? Come out of the bathroom!'

The voice of the man is now different. His shouting makes Mini quake in fear. There are lots of chores to be finished besides looking after the baby. And now all of them are lying half-done. How can she hide inside the bathroom till others return home? Outside, the man starts shouting at her with renewed energy.

The members of the family gather at the dinner table laden with many kinds of food. Everybody seems be in a happy mood. The conversation flows effortlessly. All of them treat the head of the family with respect. He talks softly. There is no similarity between this man and the one in the morning. The change makes Mini even more uncertain and afraid. Perhaps she had a bad dream in the morning? No, this man who is so respectfully addressed by everybody as *Deuta* (father), who speaks so kindly, cannot be someone to be feared. She would not be treated badly in this happy house. Mini feels relieved, at ease now.

Reassured, she goes to bed in peace.

Another fine morning dawns. Soon Mini gets into the rhythm of the household. The people depart one by one, leaving the house in custody of the old man, the little baby, and Mini.

Should she go via the veranda to shut the main gate like yesterday? She had a bad dream while crossing there, she remembers, and so hesitates. She is still a bit weary of going to that corner. She tidies up the knick-knacks in the kitchen and starts to clean the gas stove. But her ears are alert like a rabbit to catch any sound of the baby waking up. Her chores finished, she enters the baby's room to check if everything is in control.

The little baby recognises her immediately though he is still half-asleep. Hugging the baby to herself, Mini feels safe. He is her shelter, he would keep her safe from her worries about the future. She sings a lullaby softly. The shadow of the bad dream disappears. Though she is petite and carrying the baby for a long time is a tad difficult, she does not feel tired.

'Hey girl! Let me hold the baby. You go, make me a cup of tea.'

The man's hairy arm touches her breast, her belly, gropes her body as he takes the baby from her arms. She tries to burn the old man into cinder with the fire in her eyes. Instead, streams of tears flow down her cheeks. With all her strength, she pushes away the groping hands.

What are you doing? I'll tell them,' she protests.

'What do you mean? Just now the baby almost fell from your arms. If you say anything, you'll get a beating from them.'

'If you give me trouble like this every day, I'll run away. I won't stay in your house.'

'You want to run away? I'll complain to the police that you ran away after stealing things from the house. If they don't find you, they will go to your father and arrest him. You think it's so easy to run away from here, huh?'

So, she stays, but her little heart feels like a trapped

mosquito under the net. It can be attacked anytime.

In the evening, she sticks with the ladies of the house. These days she often seems disinterested in doing any chore. She is not interested in playing with the baby too and sits huddled in a corner.

'What's wrong with Mini? Why is she behaving like this?' they ask the old man.

'What to say, Boari. Today I caught her red-handed. You better leave behind only what's necessary for a day in the kitchen, daughter-in-law.'

Mini does not understand what's happening and looks at the faces for a clue. The grim faces of the women make her tremble. She moves closer to the women, trying to tell them what happens in their absence but does not get an opportunity. The secret remains with her.

'Listen girl, in this house it is I who commands everything. Nobody is going to listen to you. So, you better obey and do as I say,' the man says.

Dark circles appear under Mini's eyes. She makes mistakes. Her lullabies stop abruptly. She plays with the baby listlessly. The women in the house express unhappiness at her chores. She wants to say something but says something else. The old man looks at her with fierce eyes bidding her to keep her mouth shut. Crockery slips through her fingers and break into pieces. Even when she keeps an eye on it, the milk boils over and drips down the side of the saucepan.

The old man rebukes her, 'You have broken so many things. Who is going to forgive you? If you don't listen to me, you'll suffer.'

The afternoons become terrifying hours for Mini.

'She is a real lazy one. She sleeps all afternoon. Boari, what a stupid girl you've got for the house. Do I look after the baby, or manage her? Anyway, don't worry too much. She is still young. I'll teach her the ropes, though it will take some time,' the man says.

In the evening, Mini tries to reveal her plight to the women. But before she can do that, the head of the family goes on complaining about her faults. He gives them a list of her misdeeds. But the hypocrite also requests them not to scold Mini. She hides in the corner. At least she is saved from the abusive words. Her mistakes have been overlooked thanks to him. Whether the innocent one is trapped in the net, or is saved from the hunter, how would she understand?

Middle

'After that?'

'After that, Swargodeo, O Lord, our travels in the earth were over, our clothes became dirty. We couldn't wait there anymore.'

'Very bad, very bad. An injustice, indeed.'

'Swargodeo, what's the injustice? Stopping the story half-way or what's happening to the girl?'

'Only I have the right to ask a question, not you. You just go on with the narration.'

So, we returned home.

We got involved in the never-ending business of going on with family life. Eating, intercourse, sleeping, job, responsibilities, daily routine. Actually to be able to forget about 'should or should not' and go on living needs a kind of skill. To give oneself up to the flow of life, day in day out, night after night and crave for something called happiness. The rhythm of regular life loses its charm, meanwhile. The daily grind kills the lust for life.

We are in the same state, Swargodeo. We try to do things like you have chalked out for us but the pull of the home drags us away. We try to seek happiness as householders but memories of days gone by make us restless. Your kingdom overflows with things that should make householders the happiest people – education, wealth. But peep behind the curtain and you will find everything is a lie.

Stand on the veranda of the house where Mini stays and you will find signs of good taste everywhere. You will be compelled to admire the depth of knowledge in the smiling old man, the patriarch of the family. The walls of the house display pictures of proud scions of the family tree. But nobody is going to tell you how many Minis, Bokulis and Akonis that the cobra hiding in that tree has squeezed dry. Swargodeo! It is impossible to check every grain of rice in a pot to find if the rice has been cooked well. Doesn't the experience of Mini in her first bloom of adolescence reflect the thorns hidden under the flowers? Many Minis start their first lesson of life in such so-called educated and cultured houses. But her childhood becomes a *shahid* –martyr, even at her birth itself. Soon her golden glow of adolescence loses its purity. She loses her mental balance. It's all planned, how they become prey to lasciviousness. Sure, sometimes there are exceptions, like a few peppercorns in a basket of greens. Swargodeo, you are the lord, in your own words, exceptions are not the norm. Exceptions are just that, exceptions.

Swargodeo looks a bit crestfallen, but only for a moment. Then, keeping his usual distance from his subjects, he says, 'Those exceptions are portents of a golden future. The world moves ahead on that promise. My kingdom will go on the same way. I sent you to earth to observe the good developments in my kingdom – to bring me news of culture, industry, prosperity, the friendships and meeting of minds. But what do you do? You talk about things that have been going on for ages, that too only half the story. Like Narad, the mendicant of *swargo* (heaven). Born a pig, whenever you get an opportunity to rub yourselves in the mud, you forget the etiquette of *swargo*.'

The comparison with dirty pigs leave us fuming but we do not get a chance to protest because the lord gets up from his throne and comes towards us as if to say something. His face shows signs of anxiety.

'Listen, you don't have to report these things in the public hall. You can tell me when I am alone. That Mini girl hasn't had her menstruation yet, I suppose. Keep tabs on her. If something happens to her, we will take care of it and look after her. It's our holy duty. No one can say there is no law in my kingdom. The new law says that no one can keep a young girl like a slave. If you come to know about anything like this happening, let me know. But be careful that your queen is not around to hear about it.'

'But Swargodeo, why?'

'It's a long story. The maids in the palace are young. But they are covered from head to foot. They must feel stifled in the heat. So yesterday I pointed to my queen a pubescent girl, one of the maids, and said, "See, how she is hidden in layers of clothes. Under your initiative there has been a revolution in women's clothing. Then why should one be under veil in our own house? How can she work like this? These days the trend is to wear short dresses and work more. Why don't you start this culture in your court?" Even before I could finish, she sprang up angrily. "So, you are collecting this kind of information from your people? Listening to perverse stories of old lechers from your spies in the evening, now it has spread to you too." She said I am too old to stare at the bare legs of young girls. See? I wanted to do something good for the girls, and how things have turned against me.'

'And then what happened, Swargodeo?'

The lord straightens himself and goes back to his throne. He waits a few moments as if to catch his breath. Then in a sombre voice, he says, 'Then I woke up.'

Finale

O Lord, Swargodeo, as you know, ducklings are born from eggs even though their mother does not want to incubate. How? Hens like to incubate eggs often. But she does not lay enough number of eggs. So a clever housewife puts duck eggs in the same nest as hen eggs. So ducklings and chicks are born together. Innocent bird! She does not see any difference among the babies. So, the mother hen teaches the babies, both her own and the ducklings. Like, how to save oneself from the kites or from the wild cats. She encourages the ducklings to jump into the water while near a pond. She does not know how to swim herself but knows it is important for them. The ducklings take to water instinctively. The mother hen keeps an eye from the bank. But gradually her duty wanes. The ducklings don't care to listen to her instructions and are happily on their own in the water.

Swargodeo, this happens in the world of birds. But is it the same with us, though we too are two-legged like them? It's very different. Look at Mini. She keeps close to the women in the house when they are at home trying to share her plight. But they are more concerned with how she performs the chores. They don't see the dark circles under her eyes. They don't observe how her initial warmth has now turned into a stony silence. They don't care to find out what goes on in her mind. She is a maid after all. What has her mind to do with it? Food, clothes and shelter – she has got everything. The old man has organised books and black slates to teach her reading and writing. He is a well-known personality in the community, a pundit. So if Mini remains illiterate while living in his house it won't look nice and would be a stain on his reputation. The head of the family, who has given her shelter, food and clothes, has now become her guru. It serves a dual purpose, of course.

Suddenly, like the ducklings learning to defend themselves, Mini learns to build up her resistance. Her innocence disappears. In her little heart a formidable fort builds up, brick by brick. From the strange pages of life, she learns many cruel lessons. But she is not nervous. Only those protected by the warmth of love can enjoy that luxury. Life teaches her to be strong. The books bring to her glimpses of hope. So she enjoys reading them.

Mini looks outside. The afternoon is progressing slowly. The intense heat of midday is waning. There are also few specks of cloud. The afternoon glow paints them too. She hastens to finish the chores.

Mini is now like a habit to the family. Without her, the household would come to a standstill.

The old man wakes up from his afternoon siesta. A hot cup of tea appears immediately.

As she is leaving the room he hugs her tightly from behind. She pushes him forcefully. The red glow of the afternoon sun now gathers in her eyes.

That night, at the dinner table, the old man's soft demeanour and knowledgeable talk were missing. The members of the family look at each other, trying to fathom the source of his displeasure. Mini is no more the shy girl of yore. She serves the food, talking politely as taught by her teacher. She gives the same attention to the head of the family. But he suddenly becomes very angry. He finds some fault in her work, rises and approaches her to beat her up.

His whole family – sons, daughters-in-law, grandchildren – look on, shocked, as the dark girl with curly hair catches his arm in mid-air. Words, coated in hatred, pour out, telling the story of her exploitation. Mini was surprised at her own eloquence and audacity. The window was opening. At last, she had driven it away – the phantom fear.

The Morning Walk

Maini Mahanta

'And the river?'

'The same calm. It looks different only in the monsoon.'

'The park and the road?'

'Like before, no change. Do you want a cup of tea?'

I try to get away from Amrita's side.

'Listen! Are the vans selling fish coming still?'

'Yes, yes.'

Amrita likes to hear about these monotonous things, again and again.

The road runs by the bank of the river. Except for a few morning-walkers, usually there are not many people on the road this early. An old man stands on one leg in some

---

Original Title: Raatipua

yoga mudra, at the same spot on the footpath. The road climbs up to the end of the park. People call it Joggers' Park in the morning and Lovers' Park in the evening. A few women sit on the bench after they finish their walk. Amrita knows a couple of them. If you go ahead a little more, you will find a temple dedicated to Lord Ganesh. Devotional songs are aired from there throughout the day. By the time you arrive there, the temple priest starts the day's work by lighting earthen lamps and joss sticks. Most of the morning-walkers bow their heads when they pass by. From down the road the yelling of fishermen with their morning catch and people in big cars coming to buy the fish break the silence of the morning. When people cross this area, they cover their noses with their handkerchiefs because of the smell, a mix of fish and the bidis the fishermen smoke. But I don't mind.

Once you pass that corner, the road becomes quiet again. On the other side of the road there is the huge piece of land belonging to the water supply department. Taking advantage of the water spewing out of a pipe, a poor woman washes clothes complaining to herself all the time. Perhaps she had quarrelled with someone in the morning. Or is she mentally unstable? A healthy man wearing a white pair of shorts and carrying a stick walks by at a fast pace. Sometimes I talk with a few people of my age whom I meet regularly on the walk out of courtesy. The topics that usually crop up among us are, inevitably, blood sugar, high BP, and Patanjali medication.

'Did the fat Marwari couple come today?' Amrita asks.

Till six months ago, Amrita and I used to enjoy the morning walk together. After the doctor diagnosed me with diabetes, he advised me to go for morning walks. Amrita insisted that I go but felt lazy and desisted. Amrita decided to accompany me as an encouragement. That was the beginning. At first, when the alarm clock woke me up at 4 o'clock with its *treeng-treeng* sound, I would get irritated. Compelled by Amrita, I slogged on, yawning all the way. We didn't know about this river-side road then. One day, my friend Ajoy advised me to take the car, park it nearby and walk down the road. Now we really enjoy the ambience. An old man makes tea on a stove near the footpath. Sometimes when we have time, we sit down on the wooden bench next to him and have a cup of tea. Knowing Amrita, it was natural that she hesitated to sit on this roadside bench at first. But she later admitted that she enjoyed the black tea here better than at home.

Amrita injured herself when she slipped on the bathroom floor. She has been unable to go for the walk for a while. I don't drink tea at the old man's makeshift stall these days. On returning home, I make tea and give Amrita a cup too. The cook Sabitri comes only around 8 o'clock and then organises the chores in the kitchen. Till she became bedridden, Amrita never allowed anyone to enter the kitchen. In any case, she enjoys cooking. Now that Amrita is getting better, I am sure she would soon put an end to Sabitri's stint in our house.

'Was the 'keep away bad eyes' shop open today?'

It's our private joke, this name that we had given to the shop. In the morning, a man sits in a small shed selling strings of green chillies and lemon slices. The shop-owners buy them and hang them in front of their outlets to ill-wishes at bay. It is a superstition, of course. While growing up, we had never witnessed this kind of practice.

Without Amrita, I was unable to enjoy the morning walk. I didn't even want to go. Amrita tried to reason with me but still I balked. But when she became angry, I was compelled to go on my own. Everything was the same: the river, the park, the road. Even the people. Only Amrita was missing by my side. A few acquaintances started asking, 'Where's your Mrs?'

On returning home, now I have to describe to Amrita every detail of the morning walk. Whether the young child riding the red tricycle had come with his mother, about the man who spreads a bedsheet on the green grass in the temple compound to do yoga, or the pair of young girls who look like sisters and always whisper and giggle between themselves as if sharing some secret – everything had to be conveyed.

'These days you don't want to tell me everything,' Amrita complained.

I jumped up. Why did she say that? Was she alluding to something? To prove that she was wrong, I pulled the cane chair to her side and sat down.

'Mr Barua, the one with the stick, enquired after you today. He told me that his sister too has been bedridden with a fracture for the last three months,' I told her.

Amrita took the empty cup from my hand and kept it on the side table.

'You know, the street dogs created such a ruckus today, I am thinking of carrying a stick myself from now on,' I added.

'Did the hostel warden with her dog come today?'

'Who?'

Why did Amrita ask about her? Why?

'I mean the warden of the girls' hostel, the one who walks with her dog on a leash.'

'By the way, do we have vegetable or fish in the fridge for lunch? Otherwise, I'll go get something from the bazaar,' I changed the subject.

'Have you forgotten? Only last evening you went to the bazaar. The fish is yet to be cooked,' Amrita reminded me.

Did I look unusually pale? Was that why Amrita was looking at me so curiously? I unfolded the newspaper to hide my face.

'There's something,' Amrita said.

'What?'

What was she going to say? I lowered the newspaper. I couldn't look at her directly. Was she hinting at something concerning me?

'Zina called. She says she has got involved with a boy in Delhi.'

'Really? What does he do?'

I felt as if a huge stone had been lifted from my chest. What a fright I had! Our only daughter Zina is a Supreme Court lawyer. If she has chosen her life partner for herself it's good news, indeed.

'She says he is her colleague.'

'Good. It'll be nice to see her married soon.'

Much relieved, I opened the newspaper.

'I think I'll be able to go for the walk from tomorrow,' Amrita said.

'Are you sure? We must consult Dr Chakraborty first.'

'But he said I could when we saw him last time.'

However much I tried, something had changed in the rhythm of my daily routine, lately.

I have led a strictly regulated life all through. My childhood was bound by discipline, from brushing my teeth in the morning to evening prayers. Good books, refined films, and no addiction of any kind during my youth. And then followed a conjugal life built on love, faithfulness and responsibility. With our daughter we have led a happy life. Never was there any disturbance in this arrangement. Just as I had told my mother about Chayanika who exuberantly thumped my back and expressed her love for me in college, so also I had told Amrita about my secretary Neera, who came to my room more often than necessary, expecting a quick promotion.

Amrita is even more meticulous about discipline and punctuality. Our daily life goes by the clock. Breakfast at 9 o'clock, office, and then at 6 o'clock evening tea together at home. If I was late for tea, Amrita called me at office.

After my recent retirement, a new routine has been worked out by Amrita, adding one more hour of sleep. Later, forty-five minutes of morning walk as advised by the doctor.

After Zina left for Delhi, we had become almost like two robots. The clock kept watch on everything we did, precise and with no deviation. When Amrita gave me the cup of tea in the evening, even with my eyes closed I could tell that the time was between five to ten minutes past 6 o'clock. Life went on like this for months, years. There was nothing new to talk about between us two. So, we followed the routine – walking together in the morning, having lunch and dinner at the right time; after a month or so, going to visit Amrita's brother at his Dispur home or to my nephew's house in Noonmati. We conversed little during the morning walk too. We observed people and profiled them. Sometimes our mental images matched. Our imaginary profile about Bidisha matched somehow.

Bidisha! Often seen in black track-pants and a white T-shirt, with her dog on a leash. Amrita had commented that she looked like the strict warden of a girls' hostel. Slim, walking at a fast pace while her hair tied in a ponytail swung from side to side, she looked like a young woman in the mid- 20s from behind. From the front, her face looked older and radiated a distinct personality.

One day, we saw that she was coming out of the girls' hostel of the government college. So she was a hostel warden after all! She smiled politely. I smiled back. I don't know if Amrita did or not. Usually, she doesn't think it is good manners to smile at anyone without knowing the person. If I do so, she gets irritated and vents her opinion in no uncertain manner.

The second time I met her was after Amrita's accident. An amusing thing happened. That day Bidisha's dog sat down suddenly on the road refusing to move. Bidisha pulled him with the leash but he kept sitting there. I stopped at the sight of the tug of war between the dog and the owner. But Bidisha laughed without looking flustered (I came to know her name only that day after talking to her).

She had a pair of intelligent, but frank eyes. A tuft of hair that escaped the ponytail, covered a side of her forehead. She talked without any self-consciousness or shyness. Bidisha!

The next day I went to the top of the hill. In Amrita's company, I didn't climb this far. The doctor has told her not to since she suffered from arthritis. Tired, the morning-walkers usually take some rest after arriving at this spot. Some do *pranayama* sitting on the huge block of stone lying there. Leaning on the iron railing at the edge of the hill, I was looking at the rising sun. The sky looked like a canvas coloured by a skilled painter. Bidisha came from behind and wished me good morning. We chatted a bit and she told me that this place looked different in the evening. Whereas now you could see people like us doing yoga or exercise, in the evening the place was filled with lovers. Instead of chants of Om, you can hear intimate whisperings. I asked her if she came here in the evening too. She said she used to but she found quite a few girls from the hostel with their boyfriends there and they got embarrassed when they saw her and so she had stopped. Bidisha laughed aloud when she said that.

Next day too, I met her at the same place. I enjoyed the chitchat. Sometimes Bidisha came late, by which time I was about to return home. She said that she didn't like a life dictated by the hands of a clock. Sometimes if she didn't feel like it, she just relaxed. She would send a leave application to the college on such days and would lie stretched on her bed the whole day, listening to music. She had a relationship for a year and then got married but her husband didn't approve of her lifestyle and divorced her. According to Bidisha, people should live life with full enjoyment. She hated to be bound by strict rules.

'Aren't you going for your shower? It's almost 10 o'clock,' Amrita reminded me.

I usually drink a cup of black tea with a biscuit after taking my shower. Earlier, I did not need to be reminded of this. I tried to act natural. As usual, I had lunch at 12 o'clock, from 1 o'clock to 2 o'clock I lay on the bed even though I couldn't sleep. In the afternoon, I went to the terrace to collect the clothes Sabitri had washed. In the evening, I asked Amrita if I should help her to exercise her legs. She said no, she could do it herself now. She was able to walk pretty well by now. She wanted to come for the morning walk with me from the next day. The doctor too told me last week that she could resume her walk. In fact, she should go back to her schedule slowly, he had said.

'Would you like paneer curry with tomato?' Amrita asked.

'Isn't Sabitri coming today?'

I fussed as I saw Amrita in the kitchen.

'If she cooks, she spends double the amount of ingredients,' Amrita replied as she chopped the tomatoes.

I could see that Amrita was absolutely fine. From tomorrow she would accompany me on the walk. I felt restless. In a way, it's nothing. Yet, I tried to think back on the last few weeks when I started going alone. I let her do the cooking and went out to the veranda in the front of the house. The flowerpots that looked neglected when Amrita was bedridden now looked cared-for again. So, Amrita has been able to take control of all the chores she did so meticulously. Yes, she would accompany me in the morning from tomorrow.

Again, I felt something stirring inside me.

One day, I had asked Bidisha if she would like to have a cup of tea at the old man's shed near the footpath. She took the offer readily and sat on the bench. Another day, she bought two cups and offered me one. I had started to park the car near the hostel. Sometimes Bidisha came out of the hostel at the same time, sometimes I met her when returning to the car. Of course! She doesn't set her schedule by the alarm clock like us. She gets up when she pleases. Life should not have too many restrictions, she had said, an attitude that was exactly opposite to mine and Amrita's.

Is this opposite quality what drew me to her? Sometimes I meet her sitting on the stone slab on the road and we walk back together, talking. Bidisha said that most people spend their lives being governed by convenience of others. It's something that makes her feel claustrophobic. When she says goodbye, she says, 'Have a beautiful day' or 'Have a good day'. On the days I don't hear those words I feel gloomy throughout the day. I start the car and then look towards the hostel, waiting.

'What are you doing in the dark?'

Amrita switched on the light.

'Come, dinner is ready,' she said.

I ate mechanically, went out to lock the gate, and retired to the bed.

Amrita shut the door of our bedroom and kept her sports shoes next to mine.

From the cupboard she took out the salwar kameez suit she usually wears for the morning walk and kept it on the shelf next to the bed. Like she used to do earlier. She did not believe in wasting time in the morning. Now she switched off the light and climbed into the bed. I tossed from side to side restlessly.

'Oh, I forgot to tell you something.'

I looked at her face in the dark.

'What?'

Amrita asked, yawning.

'Dr Chakraborty has advised that you should wait for another ten days or so before resuming your morning walk.'

Oye Nathuram!

Ratna Bharali Talukdar

Oye Nathuram korili ki karma
Bapujik mari toi korili adharma
Hey Nathuram, what have you done?
You have sinned, killing Bapuji

It is said that on the midnight of 1947 at the cusp of 14th and 15th August when our country attained *swaraj* (independence), Gandhi Bapu confined himself to a small room and wept silently. It is also said that there was no kind soul around him at that time to brush off his tears. On that night of freedom, the earth under the newly born Bharat shook fearing two bloody streams flowing across the land. The blood of both shared the

---

Original Title: Oye Nathuram!

same quality – red in colour and salty to taste. Even then they gave them two names – Ram and Rahim.

It is said that, that moment, so eagerly sought with great hope by millions of people, was also washed in bitter hatred. The two rivers flowing in this acrimonious situation flooded Bapu's heart. He was, after all, the Father of the Nation. Ram and Rahim were both beloved by him. That is why in the darkness of the little room that night Gandhiji found himself immersed in sadness. He could not become a *nilkanthi* like Lord Shiva by drinking the water of the river of hatred.

They let him weep and set off. At the stroke of midnight, they gifted *swaraj* to the people; the conch shells blew at that holy juncture ushering in freedom. Fireworks lighted up the sky and the streets were bright. Amidst it all, everybody received the good tidings of the birth of the nation.

It is said that they did not want people to know that Bapu was shedding tears alone. They kept it hidden. But at midnight Bapu's tears could not be dammed and it flowed like a river across the land. Those tears sometimes came in floods, sometimes as uninterrupted rain. His ever-flowing tears tweaked our conscience. His river of *karuna* (compassion), fertilised our land and a green plant of hope sprouted.

These things are heard even today. Is it true, my husband?

The question, spoken in soliloquy, was asked by old Thurimala- ai (mother) as she sat on a bed covered with a clean white bedsheet. From her room in the multi-storeyed building you can see the Gandhi Mandap standing at the top of Sarania Hill. This building is located on a plot of land occupied illegally. At these moments, when you see Thurimala-ai, you feel as if she is telling the story of Gandhiji to someone known to her all her life and now sitting next to her. Physically, she is still active but as her mind roams between the paths of awareness and forgetfulness she often loses her way. Sometimes at midnight, she wakes up suddenly. At those moments, she thinks of her husband who had passed away and talks to him intimately. Haribar Barkakati was a freedom fighter. In his lifetime she did not have the good fortune of enjoying his company much. That is why, at this age when she has endless leisure, she talks to him to her heart's content. This gives her immense pleasure. During these happy conversations, Thurimala-ai discusses with her husband about his revered Gandhiji.

Thurimala Barkakati had faced many tests in her life. Her son brought her to stay with him in the city only recently. The village she had lived in all her life had been eroded year after year by the floods and eventually the houses were swept away. During his lifetime Gandhiji's follower Haribar Barkakati had gone to jail many times and suffered atrocities at the hands of the police. When he heard that Gandhiji sat alone shedding tears on Independence Day, he too felt the pain.

Even after Independence, Barkakati did not feel that his duty to the nation was over. He left the task of looking after the house and his son to his simple, softhearted wife. He then put his heart and soul into contributing to the building of the newly independent nation. Thurimala found it difficult to cope with the new responsibility thrust on her. She had to mortgage the only plot of land she possessed to educate their son.

After suffering from a long spell of gastric ulcer, and without getting proper treatment, Haribar Barkakati eventually left this world. Despite the penury at home, Thurimala-ai's son managed to do well in his school exams. But while studying in a Guwahati college, he somehow deviated from the path and dropped out of college without completing his graduation. He sold off the remaining land in the village and with the money started his own business and He carved a path to success, albeit dishonestly. He became like Ajamil, the despicable character, a son of Brahmins, of olden times.

Thurimala-ai always followed the idealism of her departed husband and did not maintain contact with her son. She depended on her neighbours to eke out a living rather than shift to the house of her son with her daughter-in-law and grandchildren.

By now, her son had become notorious as a land

mafia boss. With the help of his hired gang of anti-socials, he had taken hold of a plot of land not far from the Gandhi Mandap on Sarania Hill and built a huge house. Meanwhile, the court ordered that any government land occupied illegally had to be cleared. There was a huge scandal involving Thurimala-ai's son. The administration demolished many illegal buildings on Sarania Hill. This was when he brought his mother from the village to live with him. She now lived in a grey world between the present and the past. Her son put forward his case to the officials, stating that his mother was the widow of a freedom fighter and her deceased husband was the recipient of a *tamrapatra* (copper plate) in recognition of his contribution to the freedom movement. The plea saved his house from demolition. He was happy enough with his good fortune to arrange a separate room for his mother; a bed with a clean white sheet, maids to look after her, and good food and medicine.

Thurimala-ai had two grandsons. The younger one had already made a name at an early age as a heart specialist in an Ayurvedic institution in Delhi. He hardly visited his home. The older one was confined to a room on the top floor, living in a haze of drugs. His long hair was in dreadlocks, and he smelt of unwashed clothes and urine and faeces. The blue veins under his skin looked like a fisherman's net. Occasionally when he emerged from his drug addicted stupor, he cleaned himself up with his thumb, brown with burn marks from repeated burning of rolled foil paper containing the white powder drug. But despite his wayward life, he managed to get a girl who chose to marry him. Even though Thurimala-ai's daughter-in-law was fully aware of her son's looming death, living in such conditions, she teamed up with her daughter-in-law to open a women's hostel on the top floor of the house, and run a business in drugs and prostitution.

With her senses swimming between reality and dreams, Thurimala-ai was unaware of these nefarious activities. The sorceress of dementia, with her thick hairy fingers had picked up some happy moments from Thurimala-ai's life to occasionally accompany her even though she had already prepared a resting place for her not far from there. In her loneliness, Thurimala-ai was often found talking to her husband and Gandhiji.

In a way, coming to live with her son was a blessing. For, not far from her room, she could see the quiet, open space of the Gandhi Mandap. Next to it, on the stone pedestal built in memory of him, stood the white full-sized statue of Bapu. When she looked at his life-like statue with his trademark sandals, the shawl blowing in the air, the bag for alms in his left hand and the walking stick in his right, Thurimala-ai often thought that he looked as if he was once again ready to launch a *padayatra* – the long march he often took for the betterment of his people. In 1946 when Gandhiji visited Assam, the newly married Thurimala was just 14. She had accompanied her husband for the rare privilege of meeting Bapu. She had considered it as good as arriving at a famous pilgrimage centre and from then on accepted her simple, poverty-stricken life as her destiny.

Her son had now taken the advice of the doctor who looked after Thurimala-ai and arranged for a domestic help to take her for a walk regularly. With him holding her arm, every morning and afternoon she went to the Gandhi Mandap and spent some time in Bapu's company. As soon as she came to the bend in the road from where his statue came into view, she felt a sense of serenity. When he was alive, she had often discussed the life story of Bapuji with her husband. It gave her immense pleasure. She had the same feeling of fulfillment when she was near him at the mandap.

When the sculptor was carving this huge statue, did he imagine Gandhiji as a doorkeeper of people's conscience, she wondered. Would he have imagined that one day people would gallop past him like mad horsemen without seeing him? Was Bapu's heart constricted by the tears of those who were trampled under the hooves of the horsemen? She often wondered if he could see things that he did not want to see and the sights that would have pierced his eyes like poisoned arrows. The genteel folk, who came in the mornings and afternoons to pay homage to him, or those who stepped on the soft, cool grass on special days like Gandhi Jayanti to offer flowers, seemed too busy and distracted. Did anyone come here to sit for a while and ponder on his thoughts and philosophy, she wondered, as her unfocused eyes looked up at the face of the statue.

Somehow, sitting there, Thurimala-ai felt as if in the lonesome silence of the hill, Gandhiji was seeking someone to share his thoughts and tell untold stories. Was it because of this that his face had become a little shrivelled, bereft of softness? She heard many morning-walkers commenting, 'Look, how the sun and rain have eaten away at his face to make him look stern.'

Hic, hic, hic.

Thurimala-ai's meandering thoughts were rudely disturbed by the discordant sounds coming from the upper floor of the house. She got up unsteadily from her bed. Did a deer get trapped in the fangs of a hunting tiger? Had the night been sullied, cut into two by a sword bloodied with debauchery? She became very agitated. By way of solace, she hummed a few lines about Gandhiji that came to her mind:

Bapujir upasanar somoy etia hol
Dhire dhire Bapuji mandireke gol
Heno samoyate Nathu monote gunila
Upoyukta somoy booli guli eta dila
(It was now prayer time for Bapuji

Slowly, he went towards the temple
The right time, Nathu thought,
For the shot)

Gandhiji had placed Ram and Rahim equally in his heart, which angered a group of people, that included Nathu. He was waiting for his chance when Bapu left for his prayer meeting. He bent to touch his feet and at that moment let loose three bullets. Bapu collapsed on the floor. His life ebbed away as the people who had gathered for the prayer meeting ran helter-skelter in confusion. The tears that had flowed from Gandhiji's eyes on the midnight of *swaraj* was now like two streams that had dried up. When his body was put on the pyre of firewood at the cremation ground even those two streams ended up in ashes. The mourners filed in an unending stream to collect a speck of the ash. From the tears of the companions and the devastated common people, a new wave of sentience emerged to shake Bharat. Each wave, like a snake crawling sluggishly under the midday sun, entered the consciousness of the people. A deep sadness, resentment left unspoken, and a horror of the coldblooded assassination, touched the hearts of the people.

The search for a greater consciousness, a more fulfilled life that bestowed Bapu with the depth of the sea, had now been destroyed by a cruel death spewed from the hard metal, but it also ensured that he lived in people's memory forever.

They also sensed it, as if stirred by the lashes of someone whipping them on the back. Determined to build a new India, with a new consciousness, they vowed to make Gandhiji an eternal symbol.

To make sure that people in general would remember Bapu all the time, they made it compulsory to hang a picture of him everywhere. So, his portrait adorned the walls of police stations, government offices, schools and colleges. The open fields were named Gandhi Maidan. Full-size statues of Gandhiji, as well as smaller ones that were chest high, were a common sight in every public garden. Plaques in his name were in the streets of every city and town. Gandhi's philosophy of non-violence was so influential that they decided that the currency of free India should carry his portrait. Foreign tourists came to experience the Gandhi charisma.

And thus Bapu became the representative of people's consciousness, free India's conscience and our guardian of morality. They made Gandhi easily accessible to the people.

This is how it is described sometimes, isn't it, my husband? Thurimala-ai whispered to her husband as if sharing a secret. Is it because he is so easily available that people don't have any desire to sit down a few minutes and listen to his words attentively?

She now felt very tired. For a long time she sat silently. Slowly her eyes closed.

And then dawn broke.

A soft breeze blew from Sarania Hill. The air was sweet with the perfume of Tagar and Chameli flowers blooming in the open space in front of the mandap. The branches of the trees looking up to the sky now stirred with the calls of birds. With them, butterflies and bees bowed to the rising sun to welcome the new day. Slowly the horizon brightened with colours to announce the morning's arrival. The dewdrops clinging to the dubori grass at Bapu's feet reflected the sun's rays and shone like pearls.

As always, Bapu eagerly welcomed the dawn, drawing on its calm energy, as if getting ready to deal with the new day.

At this moment Thurimala-ai was seen coming towards the mandap with the help of a walking stick, accompanied by the domestic help. Morning-walkers who negotiated the two and half kilometer winding path to the mandap were about to reach too. As soon as they stepped into the open field, they would turn towards the river Lohit that flowed by the city and do their *pranayama*. After completing their physical exercise, like the morning birds, they would chirp and chatter among themselves, talking about various subjects. After their talk, they would perhaps look at Gandhi's statue, which looked as if he was ready to go on another *padayatra* and comment nonchalantly, 'How sad! The sun and rain have battered his face to make him look stern, hasn't it?' And then they would leave.

Thurimala-ai reached Bapu's statue. Perhaps she was thinking of singing a few lines from the *Ramdhun* that Gandhiji had loved so much. But at that very moment loud laughter coming from the foot of Gandhi's statue pierced the calm of Sarania Hill. Thurimala-ai jumped up in shock. She leaned on the arm of the domestic help and prevented herself from falling down. Both of them saw that on the pedestal at Bapu's feet was her grandson's wife, half-sitting and half-lying down in a vulgar position. Around her were a few young men and women. The domestic help saw that the girls were boarders at their house. Perhaps after a night of debauchery they had come there to enjoy some fresh air. The group of young people looked tired, perhaps due to their all-night shenanigans and sleeplessness. Thurimala-ai's grand-daughter-in-law was trying to keep the energy up by cracking vulgar jokes as she sat with her legs spread out in a suggestive manner. She looked like a witch with remnants of last night's make-up and signs of all-night depravity on her face. Her grating laughter destroyed the calmness of the beautiful morning. One of the boys tried to control his laughter but instead threw up at the feet of Bapu. The yellow slimy stream of his vomit trickled down from Gandhi's feet of stone.

The scene was so monstrous that even the domestic help could feel his hair stand up in revulsion. He quickly led Thurimala-ai to a spot behind the statue to hide her and kept himself hidden too. By now a few of the morning-walkers arrived. They were dumbstruck by the scene in front of them. They stood as if unable to move perhaps wondering whether one of the young men had a sharp dagger or, a pistol perhaps? It took them some time to recover. A few bold ones started to question the young people. They told them not to sully the hallowed ground of Sarania Hill's Gandhi Mandap with their loutish behaviour and asked them to leave immediately. Thurimala-ai's grandson's wife challenged them. Some of the morning-walkers took out their mobile phones to call the police. Now the whole gang became very aggressive.

Luckily, at that moment the police arrived. The morning-walkers were surprised to see that they had also brought along a few reporters. How could all this happen so fast? Who had informed them, the morning-walkers asked each other. Meanwhile, seeing the police, the woman signalled to the young men and women to disperse. They vanished down the narrow path running through the undergrowth of the hill.

On her own now, Thurimala-ai's grand-daughter-in-law became even more obnoxious. By the time the policemen and the reporters reached the spot, she had taken off most pieces of her dress and was almost naked. She wept copiously and swearing by the name of Gandhi, said that she had come for a morning walk. Finding her alone, the morning-walkers had misbehaved with her and physically abused her, she alleged. Tears flowed down her cheeks as she said the same thing to the reporters. Her flawless acting astounded the morning-walkers. After the reporters interviewed them, all of them were taken to the police station.

Silence now prevailed at the Gandhi Mandap. After everybody left, the domestic help came out from his hiding place and took Thurimala-ai back home.

News of the woman being molested by a group of morning-walkers became a sensation in the media. As the incident was also related to the Father of the Nation and his ideals, the news became the topic of discussion. It seemed as if after a long time, Indians were shaken into righteous indignation. The incessant coverage in the media made them look beyond his image on the currency notes and frames on the wall, to introspect once again about his philosophy and idealism. People started discussing the subject incessantly on the street, at lunch break in the office and during evening walks. The media also searched and found persons who still believed in the idealism of Gandhi. They were interviewed and the administration was criticised for allowing the Gandhi Mandap to deteriorate into such a filthy state. All this resulted in a new wave of awareness and a desire to look inward among the common people. Even those who had never bothered to climb the winding path to Sarania Hill to visit the Gandhi Mandap, or had any desire to breathe

the fresh air among the trees, now felt an urge to do so.

The day that started on an ugly note now saw the sun, like an exhausted carrier with a huge bag on its back, bending double and walking towards the west to take leave of the day. By that time, a new-born consciousness had entered people's hearts, and they were rearing to break into a gallop like a full-blooded horse. From the mandap and towering over the field, surrounded by the stench of dried-up vomit, Gandhi observed it all.

Batore dubori, moi pelao uvali
Gandhi ahibo buli
Gandhi ahise, podulit bohise
Anagoy shoare bori
(I clean the weeds in the front yard
Because Gandhi is coming
Gandhi has arrived, he is sitting in the forecourt
Go welcome him, with utmost respect)

Evening fell. As Thurimala-ai sang a song in praise of Gandhi in her room in the house of her unworthy son, her soft voice travelled across Sarania Hill. The kites, with wings the colour of straw, flew in from the garbage dumps in the city and perched on the branches of the trees on Sarania Hill. A death-like silence descended on the Gandhi Mandap. Darkness covered everything, but only for a few moments. Soon the sky was filled with clusters of stars like bunches of ripe Dimoru fruit. Amidst them, the moon, looking like a copper plate, happily moved to the rhythm of an enticing tune. Competing with the stars, the plains and hills of the city lit up with myriad lights. The Guwahati-Shillong Road, Moniram Dewan Path and Mother Teresa Path looked as if they were wearing garlands, shining with diamonds and myriad precious stones.

Against this air of abundant pleasure, the dark silent ground of Sarania Hill seemed to wait uncertainly. Slowly, Bapu stepped down from the pedestal. Like on other nights, he walked fast with his walking stick in hand. With the same enthusiasm that marked his walk before bullets pierced his chest, every night when others slept, he stepped out of the hard metal cover of the statue, to reach out to his beloved people, to give solace with his caring touch.

As the trees on Sarania Hill saw Gandhi getting ready for his night tour, they bowed their heads respectfully. A soft breeze emanated from the hill. The blooming Tagar and Chameli flowers perfumed the air.

Bapu descended by the winding paths of Sarania Hill. He walked down the pothole-filled road towards Ulubari. The garbage on the roadside soiled his feet. The suffocating air coming from the houses seemed to stand like a wall in front of him. He reached the Kasturba Ashram on the Sarania-Ulubari junction. There, wrapped under darkness, the dark waist-high statue of Rashtramata

Kasturba was sitting with her head bowed. On her neck was a dried garland of marigolds that somebody must have hung some time ago. Sun-rain-dust had dried the garland and now it looked like a hangman's noose. Bapu could not bear to look at her. His heart heaved with sadness. He absorbed the heartache and aimed towards Paltan Bazar walking below the Ulubari flyover.

He climbed the over-bridge of Guwahati Railway Station and stepped onto the platform. The people who did not have houses and spent the day foraging for left-over food, rested here at night. Some of them were thieves and some others were involved in illicit activities. They had often been inmates at the jail. Their chests were like perforated honeycombs, ravaged by tuberculosis. The air over the platform bore the germs of spit and cough. Sometimes the night was pierced by a scream as they went into a corner and left behind their sperm. The currency notes that they earned by illicit activities bore the blurred image of Gandhi.

Bapu arrived at midnight. His hands were like fans made of soft cottonwool as he touched their faces. Before *swaraj* was achieved, Gandhi had told the white sahibs with pride that once free, the people would decide their own destiny. That is why he had great affection for these people without a roof over their heads. He treated these people, who spread out their bed on the dirty, germ-laden platform for the night, like a father comforting a child. Comforted by his caring touch their eyes closed in welcome sleep.

Bapu now walked towards the Brahmaputra riverside. Like the orphaned crowd in the railway platform, people were waiting eagerly for him on the footpath in front of the Sukreswar temple. He did not disappoint them and offered them solace. As he left the place, the melting moonlight and the smell of tuberoses that were sold in the stalls in front of the temple, greeted him. In the moonlight the perfume of the flowers spread to the white sands on the bank of the Luit.

Not far from there at the Kasomari ghat, from the floating disco called Kamakazi, a mix of pulsating music, wild dancing and smell of alcohol made the night come alive for pleasure-seeking customers. At the entrance leading to the inner venue the rupee notes with Gandhi's picture floated in the air like white ants with newly sprung wings. Bapu felt his throat go dry with thirst. He thought of drinking from the river Luit and climbed down the promenade, skirting the river near the Kamakazi disco. It created a dark shadow and looked like a vicious giant. Suddenly, a man rushed out from the disco and ran, almost knocking down Bapu. After he disappeared, a thin body emerged, groaning. The *mekhela*-like wrap had slipped down from her torso. From her lifeless vagina a purple stream of blood flowed down her legs, an indication of the hellish storm her body had experienced.

She dragged herself to the sand and collapsed in front of Bapu. Around her were strewn crumpled rupee notes with Bapu's image. The runaway abuser had thrown them at her in his hurry. With immense care, Bapu arranged the clothes around her body, collected the notes and hid them in her clothes, drank a few sips of water and went up to the bank.

There, he saw, the police station of Fancy Bazar. As Bapu walked towards the Bharalu river, a group of young men got down from an expensive car. They brought out pistols from their pockets and fired into the air. Hearing it, the homeless people sleeping on the footpath were shocked into wakefulness. Among them was a girl called Sita Gurung, a beautiful girl with the complexion of milk and turmeric. She was from upper Assam. A truck driver from outside the state had lured her with the promise of marriage, but midway through the journey abandoned her. Hearing the sound of firing, the policemen from the station, where Gandhiji's portrait hung on the wall, rushed out. But when they saw the arrogant boys with guns, they did not know what to do. The men searched among the homeless group of people with hunters' eyes and then picked up Sita Gurung and threw her into their car. Before leaving, they threw a few notes, which bore the picture of Bapu. The policemen started picking up the notes. The homeless people looked longingly at the money.

Bapu lost the desire to continue. His journey for the night was over. On the way he peeped into the police station at Paltan Bazar. The quarter was silent now after the ruckus created by some members of the media with the false story of the events on Sarania Hill. Nobody was there. He started walking fast. Huffing and puffing, he reached the compound of the unworthy son of Thurimala-ai. Through the window he could hear drunken sounds and great mirth. He went upstairs. He saw that the policemen from Paltan Bazar thana and the reporters who were present during the morning incident on Sarania Hill were being entertained by Thurimala-ai's daughter-in-law. He saw that, as at the counter at the discotheque earlier, here too paper notes bearing his image were strewn around.

Like on other nights, tonight too Bapu travelled across the city – from the railway platform, Kamakazi disco, the bank of river Luit and now to this house, and observed the rupee notes with his picture flying in the air like white ants with wings that indicate imminent death. He felt once again the pain of the three bullets Nathu had shot into his chest.

Bapu now entered Thurimala-ai's room. The old woman was mumbling stories from Bapu's life. When she saw that he himself was present, she felt a deep sense of peace settling over her. With immense kindness, Bapu closed her eyelids with his fingers. At that moment, the light of life went out of her body and placed itself on Bapu's palms. He took it with great care and came out of the room and then offered it to the sky above.

Ai became another star among the myriads above. Bapu looked at it and smiled and then he entered the hard cover of the statue.

He once again became a statue for the next day.

Some days passed. The incidents of that morning on Sarania Hill had repercussions across the society and the government was compelled to take action. They took up a project to beautify the grounds and turn it into a tourist spot. The path to the hill was laid with concrete and smoothened. The whole road was lighted up. A guard post was created to prevent illicit activities. The museum, which was closed to the public till then, was opened for visitors.

One day a morning walker was enticed to enter the police beat-house and later, unable to bear the shame to her reputation, she set on an unknown journey. Gandhi had seen the worn-out body floating down the river on one of his night journeys. The news got lost in the pages of the newspapers and did not attract much attention from the readers.

Meanwhile, the Gandhi Mandap got a new lease of life. The number of morning-walkers increased considerably. As soon as they arrived, they faced the river and did their *pranayama*; a few did some exercise, and like the chirping birds in the morning they talked and chattered, exchanging news.

And on one of these days, someone perhaps would comment, looking up to the huge statue of Gandhi, 'Oh, oh! Look how the sun, rain and wind have attacked Bapu's statue to make him look stern, don't you agree?'

The lyrics mentioned in 'Gandhi's Geet' have been taken from the book *Asomiya Akhyan Geet Sangrah* by Bhabaprasad Chaliha, Published by Asom Prakashan Parisad

Reflection

Leena Sarma

Among the things I had brought with me, as a new bride, to my in-laws' house was Aijoni. Before you ask me, who is Aijoni, let me clarify; she is a golden-coloured plump cat with eyes ringed in black. People say she is not a local breed. Perhaps some foreigner, a tea garden manager departing the country, when leaving behind his *desi* memsahib also left behind his 'foreign' cat. Aijoni could be the daughter of that abandoned cat. How she arrived in our courtyard is a story my mother repeats many times. That night, she had finished washing the kitchen utensils and as usual, when she went to the backyard to throw away the dirty water into the field, she heard a meowing. A little kitten emerged and ensconced

Original Title: Pratikriti

itself between her legs, as if seeking protection. Under the silver light of the full moon, my mother saw a tiny golden kitten. It showed no sign that she intended to go anywhere else soon.

The next day when I saw her, I literally jumped in joy. Immediately I named her Aijoni, little darling, a name I had saved for the sister I had hoped for but who never arrived. People called me Majoni, little mother, and so my sister had to be Aijoni, right? So what if she was not a human being? Frankly, I was not a little girl at that time. I had actually finished college and was soon to enroll in the university. But perhaps because I was an only child, I was not very mature. My parents indulged me a lot. They gave in to my many demands, even if unreasonable. Aijoni was given fish for every meal, I would carry her everywhere with me, even on visits to my friends' houses.

Within a year Aijoni became a big, plump, cat. I treated her like a human being and if anyone referred to her as 'that cat', it offended me. One day my mother casually said that if she gave birth to a litter, it would be difficult to manage its brood with food and all. It was a practical problem she was talking about. But when she said that once she became a mother she would have less time for us, as she would be busy with her kittens and sometimes to protect them, she could even become violent, I was shocked at the prospect. What? Aijoni could leave me? One day on the way to the university, I dropped in at the veterinary hospital and asked the doctor if she could be spayed to prevent her from becoming pregnant. He replied, 'Of course. She would have to stay here for three days, that's all. No problem there.'

The next morning, before anyone woke up, I packed her into a bag and took her to the hospital. Aijoni had to stay there for a week. I took along rice and fish curry in a tiffin carrier for her every day. My parents were rather surprised but there was nothing they could do about it. I was their only daughter. They had never refused anything I had wanted. However, my mother mentioned that without Aijoni's consent, taking away the joy of motherhood from her was not a nice thing to do and was, in fact, a sin. Ma was old-fashioned. She believed in the consequences of good deeds and bad deeds. That was not the way I saw things. For me the most important thing was to have Aijoni exclusively for myself; everything else was meaningless.

One day, a wedding proposal came for me. A good boy, good family – what else could my parents ask for? Many of my friends were already married by then. So, I was not unwilling. Dressed in new clothes and adorned with jewellery, I rather enjoyed the huge affair. The problem arose when it was time to leave for my husband's house. I would not take one step without Aijoni. I put my foot down. There is a tradition of the bride being accompanied by a maid, and things such as household goods, furniture, etc., as gifts from the parents. But a cat? In the olden days, rich parents even gave an elephant as a gift, but never a cat. Cuddling Aijoni in my arms under the folds of my new *riha,* I entered my husband Goutam's house.

My mother cried copiously as I was leaving for my new home, whether saddened by my departure or at my mad wish to take Aijoni, I was not sure. Of course, I heard the whispers. 'What will the son-in-law say? What about others in the family?' I gathered that even my father accused my mother, 'You've indulged her too much. One day, they will send her back and the cat too, you will see.' He was trying to put all the blame on my mother. I was amused. Both of them had indulged me all my life. Never had I been denied anything I wanted.

Fortunately, I did not encounter any problem in my new home regarding Aijoni. My husband Goutam accepted her as fondly as I did. Like me, he was an only child. I learnt that he had a pet dog with whom he was very close but it died a while ago. I also came to know that he had even performed *shradha* for the dog, wearing a white *dhoti-sador*, performing all the last rites as you would for a human being. So I knew that in this new house my Aijoni would not be a problem. On the night of my *phool-sajya* – the nuptial night, my husband took her along to sleep in our bed. I told him that even though my parents were animal lovers, they did not approve of sharing the bed with one's pet. 'Because their hair falls all over...' but even before I could finish the sentence Goutam said, 'Our hair too scatters all over the bed, you know, the dead cells lie on the bedsheet too.'

How lucky was I find this new man in my life so understanding! I looked at his hands, fair, strong, covered with hair. My eyes travelled to his chest, full of hair, soft, visible through the half open shirt. His complexion was fair, with a yellowish tinge. He had intelligent eyes and a head covered with wavy black hair. Suddenly I wanted to touch this handsome man. I had never touched a man like that and the thought sent shivers through my body. Goutam looked at me too and our eyes met. He took my hand tenderly and covered it with his own. I felt an electric current pass through my body.

'Let her sleep first. Aijoni is still awake.' New house, new bed, with flowers everywhere. On other days even when the light was on, she would sleep peacefully. Both of us sat silently, waiting. After sometime, in the corner of the bed, Aijoni turned her body and then lay spread-eagled in her own style, and fell asleep.

Goutam now came towards me, gently, and I cuddled in the warmth of his chest. It was a new feeling, this thrill of intimacy. 'Meow, meow!' Both of us were startled.

'The cat...,' I uttered guiltily.

'Don't call her a cat. You have already given her a name. Why don't you call her by that name?'

He had said exactly what I wanted to hear! Goutam

lifted her up and she looked at him and then cuddled cozily against his chest. It was really strange. Other than me, Aijoni never liked to cuddle in anybody's lap. If anyone touched her, she ran away. But now she was comfortably resting on Goutam's chest and was already half asleep. He opened the door and stepped out of the room, perhaps to walk in the open air for some time.

Soon, Goutam was quite preoccupied looking after Aijoni. He didn't seem to have time even for me. After a few days, I asked hesitantly, 'Should I take the cat back to my parents' home?'

Goutam became so angry that I was afraid he would hit me. 'You are calling her a cat again? Doesn't she have a name? And why should you leave her at your parents' home? Aren't there people in this house?'

On the occasion of *aath-mangala*, the eighth day of our marriage, when we visited my parents' house as per custom, I mentioned to my mother that the cat was creating some problems in our conjugal life. She immediately lashed back, 'I knew it would happen. Who would like to welcome a new bride along with a cat?'

I tried to explain my problem a few times but she did not understand. When we were leaving, my mother told Goutam that they would like to keep the cat with them, explaining, 'Since Majoni has left we feel very lonely. So, it would be nice if the cat lives with us. We will have some company.'

But Goutam did not seem to like the idea. 'Ma, without Aijoni our house will also feel quite empty,' he said. 'Please wait for some time. When she has a litter, I will give you one of the kittens.'

Ma smiled. She took me aside and said, 'See what a well-behaved, nice man he is! He doesn't like to leave behind Aijoni thinking of your distress.'

In short, there was no way I could make my mother understand my particular problem. Even on our way back home, Aijoni sat snuggled in Goutam's lap. These days she seemed less close to me, as if I didn't hold much importance to her. She was a betrayer. She had left me for Goutam. Even for him, she appeared to be more important than me. When he returned from office, the first question he asked me was, 'Where's Aijoni?'

On the way back from my parents' place, I had told him about the operation done on Aijoni. He looked shocked. 'How could you be so cruel? I thought she would have a big litter and our house would be full of kittens.'

I looked at him. He was not bothered about having his own children but was worrying about the cat's kittens. He was grumpy all the way home, driving in silence. Because of the cat, our plans for a honeymoon also fell through. Lately, Goutam and I hardly talked to each other. Our discussions were limited to 'Has she drunk the milk? And the fish?' In fact, my participation in the conversation was minuscule. It was Goutam who was more enthusiastic about Aijoni.

A few months passed. I was getting increasingly petulant. Who could I blame? If I complained about my mother-in-law's behaviour or my husband's secret lover, people would listen to me. But if I complained that a cat was destroying my marriage, who would listen? To top it all, it was I who had brought her along to this house.

Aijoni usually slipped out of the bed in the morning. One day we heard a terrible scream from the backyard and then an incessant meowing. 'Aijoni, what happened to you?' Goutam extended his hands to her but she ran away to the front veranda as if she was being chased. 'Maybe she has stomachache or maybe a headache,' Goutam mumbled to himself.

A veterinary doctor, who was his friend, was sent for. He looked at the cat from a distance and diagnosed, 'Sorry, it's really serious. Hydrophobia. It's very dangerous.'

He brought a big drum and rolled it towards Aijoni. After some time when she walked into the drum, he straightened it, trapping her inside.

'You all stay at a distance. If you get infected, nobody can save you, you'll be dead. And all of you have to take preventive injections at once,' the vet said.

We called the boy from the nearby pharmacy to give us the injections. Even Goutam's parents who lived in another town, our driver, the gardener, our cook, the maid – everyone had to be injected. Meanwhile, Aijoni screamed incessantly.

'How long will she continue like this?' I asked the vet.

'Can't say. Three to four days. Sometimes it can take longer.'

Goutam hovered around the drum, looking disconsolate. He did not even bother to have a full meal.

'How can she be confined like this? Just because she has a disease, does it mean that we have to abandon her? Imagine if you were sick with an infection and I let you die little by little?'

'But she is a cat. And she is not me. We can't risk our lives for her,' I pointed out.

Goutam looked at me sadly and said, 'Aijoni is very important to me; she is a part of my life.'

'So, this cat is more important to you than me?' I asked him.

He refused to meet my eyes.

At dinner time, Goutam hardly ate anything. I forced him to have a bowl of lentil soup. He did not know that I had mixed a sleeping tablet in the soup. After sometime he would be deep asleep and I...

I had the bamboo stick ready. My mother often said that it was a great sin to kill a cat. Only if you gift someone a cat made of gold could the sin be atoned. I would make a little cat out of my necklace and give it to someone, I decided. And it would be over.

At midnight I woke up suddenly. I found that Goutam was not there by my side. How could I have fallen asleep like this? I jumped up and went outside to find Goutam circling around the drum. Hearing my footsteps, he turned and looked at me strangely.

'Have you touched her, Goutam?'

'No, but I have been thinking of taking her out of there. If she dies, we could die together.'

'Have you touched her?' I shouted.

'No, no. I am not lying. But I can't bear it anymore.'

Goutam's strong denial told me he was not lying. I took a few steps back and, taking hold of the bamboo stick hit him from behind – not very hard but enough to make him unconscious. I dragged Goutam tenderly and put him on the veranda. Now I looked inside the drum. Aijoni's eyes shone in the moonlight. Around her mouth was a layer of froth. A strange kind of moaning came from her. I picked up the bamboo stick. Perhaps it would need to be hit three or four times and then everything will be over.

I drew a small figure of a golden cat on the ground. In fact, as small as an ant.

The Smell

Juri Baruah

The whiff of beef curry was floating in the air. Those who were familiar with the smell could easily imagine the rich colour of the thick gravy. The smell travelled carelessly along the railway track. Even the Inter City train's speed could not expunge it. It didn't wait, like people on either side of the track, to let the train pass. It continued to travel on its own, uncaring. Some people waiting there tried to ignore the smell. Rudreswar the Brahmin from Padumoni village looked rather grotesque when he screwed up his nose at the smell. Manohar Lal, a compounder at the Hanuman Tea Estate, seemed unconcerned. The girl working in the new beauty parlour at the *teeni-ali* tri-junction, the one with a Shilpi bindi

---

Original Title: Gondh

on her forehead – I have forgotten her name – fiddled with her dupatta, trying to arrange it carefully. Near the parlour, the old dressmaker Hafiz-kai (we shortened *kakai*, elder brother, to *kai*), who always sat bent over the sewing machine in his shed, paused. Whether he too could smell the curry was difficult to make out from here. He looked as though he was counting the compartments of the train passing by. Only when Padmeswar, the ploughman, rang the cycle bell did he stir from his reverie and seemed to wake up to consciousness.

Consciousness? What does it mean?

Is it like the sense of smell?

Nobody can see it. Yet, even if invisible, it continues to work. It remains alive and elusive, refusing to be bound.

Like consciousness, nobody can block this smell. No rule, no policeman, no fear of jail, no temple, no masjid, can outlaw it. It goes on its way independently. So, the whiff of the beef curry did not care a hoot that it would be recognised by the people around. When it glided from the window of the Muslim house on the other side of the tracks and travelled into the backyards of houses in the Ahom colony on this side, politics did not enter its realm.

In fact, so many different smells travelled around, stark, independent – in the air – in the blast of the whistle of the trains running on the broad-gauge line recently upgraded from meter gauge, through the window of the shop standing on stilts like a *chang-ghar* on the other side of the tracks, a shop that opened only in the evening. Hasina and Pubali surreptitiously bought packets of fried green peas from there. They were greedy for the snack. The packets were bought for Rs 5 each but were worth Rs 10 to them. When she tried to peep through the window of the shop to look beyond, Hasina could get a whiff of pork curry and home-brewed rice beer. But they found the smell of the fried green peas much more enticing. Hasina's hungry eyes and Pubali's impatient fingers attacked the paper packets voraciously.

At that moment, yes exactly at that moment, did Pubali smell the beef curry on Hasina's frilled frock?They had even pulled each other's hair during a *kabadi* match when one tried to cheat. But that was soon forgotten and they raced to the hillock near the bridge, running parallel to the tracks, their hair flying, their gay laughter ringing in the air. The hillock resonated with the sound of their laughter and the bridge echoed the sound of *jhon..jhon... jhon* as a train passed by.

Their childhood was filled with many moments like these and even later their lives remained uncomplicated and rich with unquestioned friendship and laughter.

If the stall of Bapukon-*daiti*, they called him *daiti* (uncle), did not open for three or four days Hasina became worried. She could not concentrate and so lost the game of kabadi. Neither was Pubali unconcerned.

The smell of the fried green peas always beckoned her. True, they could also buy fried green peas at Putul-da's shop at the corner of the road along with other items like wooden spoons topped with tamarind paste and bubble gum. But the green peas from here did not have the same aroma. Instead, they could get the smell of petrol. Putul-da used to sell fuel in plastic bottles. The young men who rode their bikes to Borsil bought petrol from him and on their way teased the girls of the village. Putul-da did not object, he was too astute a businessman.

On Sundays, Naga women from the hills came down in groups, their cane baskets filled with bamboo shoots, pulses, dry bamboo shoot pickle, wild yam, and chilli powder. They did not stop by Putul-da's shop. They went to Bapukon-*daiti's* shop instead. He did not sell anything in the daytime during Sundays but on these days, he sold salt and soap to the Naga women. They would open the packets of Lux soap and smell it. After they left, the front yard of the old man's shop would smell of soap.

Even if Hasina tried to force her, Pubali balked at the idea of visiting Putul-da's shop. One reason was that on the bench in front of the shop, a group of men, supposed to be well informed but sadly 'unrecognised geniuses' congregated. If they saw her, they would ask: 'Tell us why the earth is round. Who first discovered the steam engine? What is meant by the Leap Year?' If she failed to answer, they would *tut-tut* and wonder aloud what was being taught at school these days? Nothing!

So, she restrained Hasina, saying, 'Forget about the tamarind chutney and Hajmola. Wait a bit, those things will be available at Bapukon-*daiti*'s shop soon.'

As Pubali predicted, these tempting things soon appeared at Bapukon-*daiti's* shop. But he hardly bothered to display them. He gave away a packet of Sargam free with green pea packets. Hasina still tried to peep into the compound beyond the window. But *daiti* would shoo them off, scolding, 'Go! Go home! Your mothers must be waiting with bamboo sticks ready.'

When he spoke, they could get the smell ofcigarette. Mingled with it was also an inner distress, a regret, which he tried hard not to show.

'The old man won't die for a while; his voice tells me.' When Pubali said that, Hasina stopped midway. Pubali too slowed down. Their innocent exuberance was overshadowed by the fear of losing *daiti.* Pubali threw her head back and poured the contents of the Sargam packet into her mouth. It tingled with the sour taste. She finished off the packet at one go and forgot that her tuition teacher was to come home later.

In the afternoon when she returned home, after roaming around the whole day, her mother dashed out of the house to confront her. Instead of the bamboo stick, she held the pointed bamboo *shola* used on her loom. Pubali did not have a chance.

'You despicable girl, so you want to roam around like a cow that has been let loose the whole day? How dare you? I have been looking for a teacher for so long and got one at last. But look at her. She is not at home when he comes. You'll bring shame to the family, I tell you. You are getting worse by the day. Don't forget that you are a girl.'

Pubali was often reminded that she was a girl. It did not bother her any more. But how could she go to meet her friends when her calves bore the marks of her mother's bamboo *shola*? So, she put the empty packet of Sargam inside the zipless pocket of her school bag and stayed home.

Rahmat Sir, who was liked by everybody, came again the next day. Pubali forgot the pain on her calves when she saw him. She removed the magazines, *Prantik* and *Mukuta,* from the table in the portico to make space for her math book. She could smell the nice *attar* coming from Sir's clothes.

At that moment Pubali remembered the *sanchi* trees in their backyard. Sometimes when he was short of money, her father sold one of them. Hasina had told her that from the tree one could make *attar*. For two days in a week, Rahmat Sir left behind the remnants of the perfume in the portico of Pubali's house. Once its smell disappeared, Pubali arranged the magazines on the table again.

Even in days later, did Pubali, her parents, grandmother and her restless brother smell the beef curry? Perhaps they did, but found no reason to object. Or perhaps they did not know where it came from. Or, even if they did, they did not mind. In all likelihood, that smell was accepted as a simple, everyday affair.

When Pubali attained puberty, for the ritual 'small wedding', *shanti biya*, according to the local custom, Ammi, Hasina's mother, presented her with a long, frilled frock. Hasina was yet to cross the threshold into puberty and unlike Pubali, she was free from any kind of restrictions.

The days when they munched on the fried green peas and roamed around or played kabadi now disappeared from Pubali's adolescent calendar. She now braided her curly, unmanageable hair. When she went to school, she deliberately went a little earlier so that the gate at the level crossing of the railway track would be closed and until the train passed she could check on Bapukon-*daiti's* shop.

The shop was there at the same spot all right. The hut tilted a bit to the side due to disrepair. The Amla tree next to it gave welcome shade. Like grandchildren to old couples.

But many things had changed, unlike Bapukon-*daiti's* shop. Pubali and Hasina witnessed many of these changes – names and characteristics, the inability to acknowledge that one can talk normally instead of raising one's voice while trying to make a point. One Sunday, when Pubali's family was having a sumptuous lunch with pork curry cooked with bamboo shoot bought from the Naga bazaar, the ploughman Padmeswar came running to inform them that Bapukon-*daiti's* only son Ananta was found murdered. Pubali's mother left the lunch midway. The pork curry cooked in the iron wok had lost its taste instantly. The news travelled quickly through the village, like a forest fire.

Bapukon-*daiti's* father was a well-known personality in the area. He had fought for India's independence. A soldier who did not dream of a land divided between Hindus and Muslims. All these things Pubali and the children heard from the discussions among the elders. The man did not ask for anything after Independence. Disillusioned, he kept on living in the same bamboo cottage. Bapukon-*daiti's* anger at his father doubled at the sight of the withered house. One day, he forced himself to question his father, 'What idealism are you talking about? What's this country you fought for where one family takes the name of a king and reigns over the subjects?'

After his father died, Bapukon-*daiti* built this shed near the railway track and opened his shop. It was an apology of a shop, selling nothing much – home-brewed rice beer prepared by his mother and pork curry. At first, the villagers passed sarcastic comments at the loss of status for the son of a freedom fighter; they criticised him and even abused him verbally. But Bapukon-*daiti* stuck to his guns. He had sold all the paddy fields they had owned to treat his ailing father. He had to earn some money to keep the home fires burning. He had to look after his old mother too. Did they want him to starve?

It was his self-defense but underneath there was also a simmering resentment. This was his way of defiance against the country, the society, the system. Bapukon-*daiti* could not take up the gun, could not go shouting slogans on the highway. He did not want to visit office after office in the town to get a job. So, he used to say, 'Let it be. I'll stay in the village and protest in my own way.' The children learnt all this when their mothers talked about Bapukon-*daiti*.

After the murder, Rahmat Sir stopped coming to teach Pubali. An overpowering sense of nervousness seemed to suck in everything around them. Except for the trains that passed by, everything else seemed to stop moving. Pubali could not meet Hasina as before. There was a time when she fought with others wanting to include Hasina in their group while dancing for the Jeng-Bihu celebrations. Pubali's aunt was yet to get married. She took out her box of multicoloured powder and put bright red dots on their foreheads. Below the big red dot, she also put a small black one to keep off the evil eye. Hasina's bun of smooth silky hair looked oversized for her small frame. She looked beautiful, but Pubali was not jealous. Rather she was proud to show off her friend when they went visiting the households in the village, dancing as per custom of Rongali Bihu.

Pubali paused, lost in the mists of memory. Memories, rich and luxurious, come to her unbidden. It is a wonder that one does not have to pay for them. They come in waves, waiting in the wings and then, like a whirlwind, churn through the mind as reminiscences. The apathetic politicized environment of our times cannot prevent them from coming.

When Pubali had wanted to go to Hasina's place for Eid, her mother did not object. She did not scold her when she wore her still new Bihu frock. As she parted her hair in the middle, Pubali peeped into the hollow of the bamboo pole in the veranda where she had cut a hole to make an impromptu saving box for money. Should she take out some money? Her father could read her mind and gave her Rs 10. Pubali's solemn face brightened instantly. She ran to Bapukon-*daiti's* shop with the money in her hand.

Today, if she could recall even fleetingly, the smell of the fried green peas and the halwa generously sprinkled with cashew nuts, she could return to her innocent childhood, something long gone, washed away by the winds of social change.

The forecourt of Hasina's house with the Bougainvillea plants now had Hasnahana flowers blooming. They filled her adolescence with their perfume. Under the starry sky she returned home, walking by the road skirting the railway track, after enjoying the Eid feast. But she and Hasina in their innocence never thought that it would be the last time they were going to be together.

The government had changed, the tone of the people's groups was changing, their problems, their arguments, even the level of tolerance and patience, were changing rapidly.

There was no way to know whether the window to Bapukon-*daiti's* shop was open or not. Pubali's brother Rontu was not a customer of that shop like Pubali and Hasina. For their group, new kinds of packets were arriving. Things that were available in the globalised world. Packets of potato chips, Kurkure, pouches of jam and jelly, brightened Putul-da's shop. The bottles of petrol had by now disappeared. In their place, there hung colourful posters, offering recharge facility for mobile phones.

But the sound of the kettledrum still came from the village temple, *namghar*. During exams, Pubali and her friends got up at the first call of the *azan* at dawn and at the sound of the evening *azan*, sat at their table to study.

For Pubali, the end of her friendship with Hasina had stemmed from Bapukon-*daiti's* son's death. At least, she blamed it for their breakup. People were slowly forgetting about the incident. But they did not cross over to the other side of the railway track as before. The path near the railway track stood as a dividing line between Hasina and Pubali. An undefined line that teaches both sides to accept 'We are different from each other.' The more that line strengthened, the more Bapukon-*daiti's* shop tilted sideways.

At the turning in the road leading to the *namghar*, a liquor shop had come up where people gathered to drink even in the daytime. That bright young man who had asked them questions like why the earth was round while sitting on a bench in front of Putul-da's shop, had now opened a *dhaba* selling liquor. The only difference was that, instead of fried *chana*, he sold chilli chicken and tandoori roti. On the huge TV screen there, you could see figures gyrating in vulgar dance moves.

These things were discussed by the women who gathered in their courtyards in the afternoon, helping each other pick grey hair or nits from their hair. Pubali eavesdropped while cleaning the chimney of the table lamp. From their gossip, came the unpleasant smell of half-burnt roasted duck legs.

'After doing so well in studies, this is what he has brought to the village!' they lamented.

'Didn't you see that day the youngest son of Pitamabar and that uncouth man, what's his name – actually we shouldn't take his name, he ogles at the girls all the time – both of them stood against the headlight of a car and peed.'

Aunt Geeta did not bother about Pubali's presence while divulging to her mother all the gossip from the next village. You could call it gossip or criticism. Talking about others kept the women happy in the afternoon, enough to keep them away from TV. But it was also a kind of warning about the future.

The warning was given to Pubali too, as also to every young girl in the village. Even in that warning, there was smell. It pertained to the body. The odour of menstruation, and at other times the aroma of Himani cream and perfume. Pubali or Hasina in their days of wild freedom could have never imagined that smell could signal the coming of a certain age.

But even then you could see, through the gaps between the coaches of the running train, all those familiar faces – Rudreswar the Brahmin from Padumoni village looking rather ugly with his screwed up nose, compounder Manohar Lal's expressionless face, the restless girl from the beauty parlour with a Shilpi bindi on her forehead, the tired eyes of old dressmaker Hafiz-*kai*, the mud-covered legs of ploughman Ratneswar and in the middle, and among them weren't there Ananta, Bapukon-*daiti's* son and his wife Arfeen?

Ananta and Arfeen did not follow rules. They did not believe in set boundaries. They did not object to any kind of smell. Was this refusal Ananta's way of protesting at the prevailing time? A time when mistakes and crime blurred the lines? The *namghar* that was built in remembrance of Guru Sankardeva's philosophy of no discrimination among people was now a place where people were talking about castes and religious divides. All of a sudden, the people seemed to get a whiff of beef curry in the air. The blessed call of *azan* that cleansed people's minds now had people stepping out with their eyes reflecting unspoken words like *kafir*.

And like this, the days were merging into a continuum of oblivion. In that state of forgetfulness, the bloated dead body of Ananta floating on the Nafuk stream became a symbol of useless protest. That evening, even the train booming over the railway track had not been able to suppress the heart-rending cries. *Namghar, masjid,* the *pundits* and *maulvis* – nobody expected to solve the problem of the tragedy of those screams. Yet they had set the rules – lived by them, kept the rules alive.

Eventually with the passage of time, these rules came to be accepted, when one day Hasina and Pubali again faced each other, standing on either side of the railway track. In their childhood, they had learnt to count the number of coaches of the passing trains. But their adolescence taught them to examine the boundary line of resentment and revenge.

When the gate at the level crossing opened, both Hasina and Pubali tried to move from their designated places. They again wanted to smell each other. And question the rules. They understood why, when the sound of the evening *azan* drifted out from the masjid, a recorded reading of the Gita-*paath* was played at high volume from the *namghar*.

Yet, nobody could hide the smell of the beef curry. They could not forget either the taste of the pork curry at Bapukon-*daiti's* shop. And thus, Pubali and Hasina were approaching a debate on 'It was not there before.'

They advanced towards each other and met again across the railway track, where there were explanations galore about the minority, the story of cow thieves was a daily topic, the story of Deendayal Upadhyaya was repeated like the Gayatri *mantra*, and the increasing divide among people was the TRP of the media. The scene on the other side seen through the gaps in the train coaches seemed to be the same, the dupatta on the girl's shoulder slipped again and again, but people were bent double with the burden of intolerance.

Pubali and Hasina took deep breaths. The smell of beef or pork was not there in their breath. That smell had lost its individual identity, forcibly layered with a tinge of saffron. That breath was on sale, the price measured on the scale of conscience and idealism. That smell was pierced, again and again, by shards of glass made of differences and dividing lines.

We had forgotten what our names were – farmer, labourer, opposition leader, lover, common man, *aam admi*, but we knew that the smell clung to our bodies, nonetheless.

We could not return to 'before' from its clutch.

Eye, That Unrelenting Eye

Moushumi Kandali

The girl, her skin the colour of a ripe pomegranate, is walking without a care, despite the pouring rain and flashes of lightning. She sings soulfully, her heart is in pain as she misses her beloved... in flashback. A scene of the rendezvous between her lover from another land and herself and then it's a 'cut' as a bumble bee sucks the honey from a flower... The scene recurs again and again in Ramananda's mind as he peddles his bicycle. He hums *kaha goyo mori bedardi balma* (Where have you gone my heartless love). The smooth leaves of the elephant apple tree shine under the silver moon, as though they have been rubbed with mustard oil.

Original Title: Sei shokutu

The afternoon sunlight was streaming through the window. Madan drew the curtains to shut out the light and then went back to bed and hugged his pillow.

Ramananda stops suddenly while passing the neighbourhood that is deep in sleep. He sees light from an earthen lamp glowing through the hole in the wall of a cottage. His eyes light up. The light moves enticingly, whispering to him – come, come here. Like a cat, Ramananda goes stealthily towards the cow-dung-covered bamboo wall and peeps through the hole. Immediately, a shiver of excitement crawls up his legs to his crotch, turning it into a hot, rigid object. Aah! There, in front of his eyes is *kabita* (poetry).

Madan is fond of poetry and even more, its embellishments. That's why his description was capped by another layer. Through it all emerged the milky moon of the *shuklapaksha*, the fortnight when the moon passes through half-light to fullness. The lonely heroine, the bright elephant apple leaves and the melting drops of moonlight. Though we felt he was going overboard with excessive detail, we listened to him anyway. What else was there to do on this hot day as the afternoon slowly advanced? There was so much time to idle away. Thankfully, this marathon session of debate and gossip helped fill the lethargic hours offering us an outlet for gratification. Or call it a necessary evil.

So, indulging in this necessary evil of an *adda*, we lazed around, sometimes lying down, sometimes leaning against the wall or squatting on the floor, smoking or crushing tobacco between our palms. And oh yes, imagining Ramananda in the mind's eye. Look, he is peeping through the hole, he is sweating with excitement and lust, he can see on the bamboo bed a pair hissing with pleasure like entwined snakes. A pair of smooth naked legs, white like elephant tusks, are swaying with the rhythm of coitus – up, down, up, down.

We too are singed by the heat as his breathing becomes faster, something creeping up and down inside akin to lightning, never mind that the presence of an earthen lamp on a moonlit night seems out of place. Perhaps there was some break in the poetic narrative, a little tripping in the rhythm, but we enjoyed it anyway, accepting that the flaw was only technical. Had the earthen lamp not been there, how could Ramananda, returning home through the silent night after the last show at the cinema, have been allured by the faint glow and then been able to enjoy the excitement of watching two people indulging in sex?

Even though there was fantasy fiction or pornographic sites that offer much more variety, participating in this kind of real experience had more authenticity. Definitely, real persons, real involvement brings with it a different level of pleasure, aided by the slow sips of liquor while listening intently to the detailed description of all that was happening. It touched a deep-rooted pulse of pleasure in all of us. So why shouldn't we soak it in? So my dear moralistic uncle, it's irrelevant for us to ask this basic question as to how Madan managed to get all these details of Ramananda's secret adventure. Like Arjun with his bow at the *mahasabha* when he won Draupadi's hand, our eyes were focused on the eye of the fish. So, in company with Ramananda, we too peered through the hole in the bamboo wall and lost ourselves in the forbidden pleasures of a voyeuristic experience.

With blurry eyes and somewhat blind to our surroundings, we were lost in a world of the known and unknown when she barged in like a blinding shaft of light or a wild west wind, shattering everything around us. Our pot of self-absorbed pleasure, which was getting thicker with constant boiling, wobbled and fell down on the cold floor. Our males-only Sunday afternoon trip was suddenly stopped on its tracks before reaching the crescendo. We were tired now; our thoughts of forbidden pleasure had exhausted us. Like the mythical Basuki snake that worked relentlessly wrapping itself around the Mandara mountain to squeeze out the *amrit* (heavenly nectar) from the deep ocean, we now desired only one thing with our whole being – the *amrit* of exquisite physical pleasure. Perhaps that's why, or because of her bright yellow dress the colour of the Taruakadam flower, or was it because our eyes were unfocused in the half-light, half-dark ambience of the room, we did not see her face. We saw an ethereal figure with a contour of peaks and valleys. Now in the sudden intrusion of light, we were like wild animals caught unaware by the piercing light from a car, standing still stupidly with eyes distended. Our silent gaze ran over her lustily only to be jolted into reality when she said sarcastically, 'It's now evening. Switch on the light and stop your male gaze.'

We laughed aloud as she uttered the words 'male gaze' and teased her, 'Are you now in the company of the gang led by Griselda Pollock, Linda Nochlin and all?' She, however, shrugged off our mocking laughter nonchalantly and jumped onto the study table, found an empty space and sat there swinging her legs. She was like that. In common parlance, irregular, an odd creature. Then, in another way, confident, straight-talking, independent. In our band of men, she is the only woman. She is our father confessor, our soul sister. But even then, one couldn't let go of everything she said, right? Bijoy couldn't either. Fencing off her sharp jibes with ironic laugher, he shouted, 'What are you harping on about – male gaze, male gaze? What's gender got to do with it?'

The lights were switched on, the Tortoise coil lit to kill the mosquitoes. Through the window an order was given to the kid working at Kalita Sweets – six cups of tea and six *goja* sweets.

The job done, Bijoy returned to the subject of the 'male gaze'. 'Why should we be blamed always for the so-called gaze? Are we the only ones who enjoy it? What about women? Don't they indulge in it too?'

It could indeed be true. If an opportunity arose, the unmet desire and lust hibernating in the deep subconscious could uncoil among women too. Don't they too want to savour with their eyes, taste with their tongues, something forbidden? Don't they pin up on the wall of their mind the alpha male's dream body, wet with sweat and water? Don't we also, like them, want to peep through the secret hole, like Ramananda, at some point of time? Yes, let's admit it, why Ramananda alone? All of us, at least once in our lives, have indulged in peeping through the hole that promises enjoyment of a different kind. Or have carried within us the desire to do so. Like wind blowing through a *sunga*, bamboo pipe to boost the kitchen fire, we have also at some time or the other peeped through an enticing hole to fan the fires of desire, sometimes going beyond even and taking off the clothing of norms that define 'should' and have warmed ourselves in the heat of the flames. Ah, what pleasure, this heat on a cold winter's night! Lovely! Pleasurable. Self-indulgent. Like the itchy skin on Seer Raikya's body. He kept scratching his skin invaded by ringworms – not once or twice, but on and on – *rokoh, rokoh, rokoh*!

Seer Raikya was sitting on the bank of the river,

scratching himself all the time, while seeking the meaning of life – the Ultimate Truth. The rough patches on his rash-covered body was reflective of the thirst for *brahma-gyan,* the ultimate knowledge, and the unending restlessness of his soul, searching and questioning the meaning of this existence. But we keep scratching our skins only to appease the desire of the body.Yet,they are like bubbles in the pond of our body and then disappear after some time. But how quickly this skin disease is spreading now! Our skins show the dry patches and we have this unbearable urge to scratch all the time.

A few days ago, we came across a modern version of Seer Raikya's story. A little child had fallen down a 60-ft-deep borehole. A child caught in a tussle between life and death. It became a thrilling game. They started telecasting the plight of the half-clad boy on live TV. His fear and suffering was exposed to the probing eyes of experts in marketing who are always on the lookout for events that draw in audience in search of thrills. They were now sitting around the edge of the gaping hole and calculating the possibilities – enjoyment and self-indulgence went together hand in hand... *rokoh, rokoh, rokoh*!

From Ramananda to the male gaze to female libido and then seamlessly to Seer Raikya's itchy skin and now the helpless little boy in the 60-ft-deep hole. Suddenly, Abinash's cell phone trilled. Bijoy lighted another cigarette. Madan got up to collect the clothes from the line outside. She snatched the cigarette from Bijoy's lips, drew at it rapidly and blew the smoke towards us. Looking disgusted, she said, 'You guys are too cynical and critical. A little child fell down in an open hole, the channels started the live telecast and see how the whole country reacted. People from all corners, never mind their caste or religion, streamed to temples and masjids to offer prayers for him. Can't you not be cynical about this simple compassionate gesture?' Her voice was seething with anger by now.

We were angry too. But not with those simple, common people who had prayed for the child unselfishly. Our anger was aimed at the dark corner behind the screen, those actors and crafty directors of the so-called drama because we saw how a story was being woven around the sad plight of the little boy stuck in the hole for two days. The central character in the play was the announcer. He was giving a running commentary on the 'event', his voice and body language fit for a live coverage of the final match of the football World Cup.

In the parallel space in the studio sat a politician, a religious guru, a Feng Shui expert, an astrologer, a traditionalist leader, a feminist, and a film star dressed in designer clothes. The latter was singing as if looking straight at the child, *tum jiyo hazar saal* (May you live for a thousand years). The anchor said – 'If you want to be a part of this campaign to save the child, please SMS to this number.' Immediately on the TV screen an SMS appeared, 'Oh you brave son of *mata dharitri* — resting in the lap of mother earth, please come up to your own mother's lap.' Another was singing over the telephone, *tum mukkadar ka sikandar ho* (you are the lord of your fate). Meanwhile, they all helpfully disclosed for public consumption their names, surnames, addresses, etc. The little child was crying as he saw a poisonous insect crawling towards him. The scene was juxtaposed with another, a close-up of a birthday party. A woman in a dark dress, lips painted with bright lipstick, her parted hair adorned with a designer *kapali* hair ornament, was cutting a cake. She was surrounded by a happy group of people wearing expensive designer dresses. She was singing 'Happy Birthday to you!' They were celebrating the birthday of the little boy still trapped in the hole. Slices of the multi-layered cake generously topped with vanilla and chocolate, the kind that little boy had perhaps never tasted, were distributed among the group.

The cigarette she had snatched from Bijoy's lips was now only a stub. She blew the last ring of smoke silently, tired, as if blowing off her disgust too. The rings of smoke disappeared into the empty air and burdened by the emptiness; we were silent too.

Frankly, we found ourselves reflecting on that crowd of opportunistic modern Raikyas, scratching the skin ridden with the itchiness of greed and self-indulgence.

A deep sense of guilt wracked our consciousness. While watching this thrilling saga of life and death, something inside us metamorphosised – without our knowledge, almost clandestinely. Watching such exciting episodes on a regular basis, and enjoying it too, our sensitivity had become crippled. Let's admit it, though starting with a certain empathy, even we don't know when it morphs into a kind of voyeuristic pleasure like a rape scene or masturbation. To cheat ourselves, we wrap ourselves in a sheet of sympathy but actually we are far from being sympathetic. We enjoy our favourite dishes, cuddle inside our warm beds and with eyes half-shut, enjoy the unfolding of death, sex, murder. And a private adventure of people like Ramananda becomes public. He stands exposed. Sure, it's a peep into forbidden territory but it's at least connected to the natural desires of flesh and blood. When manipulated by agents from the world of scratchers, this same act becomes ugly, unnatural, corrupted. A world bereft of natural law.

In this anarchic world, the sudden sound of a sharp whistle and a train's wheels *jhak-jhak-jhak* broke us out of our reverie. The night train passed by on the track outside. She stood by the open window and stared at the train speeding past announcing its presence through its arrogant whistling. On the other side of the railway tracks, the cityscape was grey and misty. The only thing that was visible clearly was a discoloured red piece of cloth blowing in the wind from the branches of the huge peepul tree, like a wounded red flag. She turned and looked at us, her face and eyes even more wounded than the red piece of cloth and asked, 'Do you remember Gudiya?'

Yes, we remembered. We remembered everything. Her kohl-lined wide eyes, the newspaper clippings on her life, everything. It was the year 1999. Just 10 days after her wedding, her soldier husband had left for the border to fight the enemy. He disappeared and the Indian army declared him a deserter. The family waited for four years and then taking him to be dead, they married her off to another man from their own community. But the husband returned the next year. He had been captured by the enemy and was jailed. The situation became complicated as Gudiya was pregnant. The village panchayat sat in judgment and ordered her to go back to her first husband, who was reluctant to accept the unborn child. To solve this problem a television channel volunteered to find a solution. For the first time in India's history, a 'tele-panchayat' was organised. There, through SMS, viewers from across the country set up an unprecedented example of participating in a reality show to give verdict on the most crucial event in Gudiya's life. Yes, we remembered well the horrific live telecast – Gudiya sitting like a statue on the floor of the studio, her face reflecting the suffering she was going through. For hours that drama of the tele-panchayat continued. Enthusiastic participants and viewers surrounded the eight-months pregnant Gudiya – the so-called respectable people, the elders, parents, religious gurus, brothers, intellectuals, the keepers of social norms. In front of Gudiya, a thousand people were watching and beyond, lakhs more. On both sides of Gudiya were the two husbands – the prize in the game of dice. The well-mannered journalist-cum-anchor announced, 'Dear people, please decide for the sake of justice, who should win the woman?' In the ensuing debate, voices justifying individual opinions rose to a crescendo. Under the arc lights of the studio and bright metallic electronic machines, the tense game moved towards a climax, perhaps more nerve-wracking than the football World Cup final or an India-Pakistan cricket match. The studio was overwhelmed by SMS messages, the telephone kept ringing incessantly.

In this highly charged atmosphere, awash with sound and light, the first husband looked visibly triumphant. After all, he was the hero back from battle. The other man was just a labourer in a shoe factory. He did not have the skill to fence with clever words of those who were sitting in judgment of his fate. He was ignorant of the fact that this was the age that valued stirring words. Silence was as dead as mother tongue, no longer used.

And what about the woman? Who was she but an object, to be auctioned at will. Who cared that she sat there hour after hour with her swollen belly? Who cared if she was exhausted with hunger and thirst? Who cared about the baby inside her? Was her head reeling under the stress of sitting under the piercing studio lights and among the cacophony of sounds? But where was the time to pay attention to these trivialities when the game was on? For, in this people's court seeking to set an example of justice, these small things did not matter. More important issues were being examined: the administrative machinery, political leadership, the defence forces, multinational companies, the powerful fourth estate holding up the pillars of the democracy, etc. Where was the place for minor issues like hunger, thirst, love, individual's rights in this debate?

Anyway, at last, the moment of climax arrived. When, through the novel process of electronic messages sent by lakhs of invisible people, the verdict was given that Gudiya should go back to her first husband. A huge celebration erupted on the city streets. Processions were taken out, fireworks lit up the sky, the particular channel's TRP rating soared, and the representatives of multi-national companies which sponsored the event smiled in satisfaction.

After this long entertainment show, we retired to bed exhausted. Gudiya too found relief in the *khatia,* the make-do bed made of criss-crossed rope. But was she left in peace? Not at all. A group of women surrounded her as if she was an animal at the zoo. In the doorway, a group of men kept watch. Media persons came in and out as also did many other people. The hero moved among them, his mobile phone constantly plastered to his ear as he received congratulatory messages. He told someone, 'I'll let the baby be with the mother for a few days after birth. After that it will be sent to the real owner.' He smiled proudly at this show of his quality of the milk of human kindness. Amidst this noisy melee, Gudiya lay on the *khatia* listlessly, her eyes dull and lifeless. People saw the woman lying like this but they did not see Gudiya. They did not bother to wonder why she was supine like that, a woman who did not suffer from any illness. After two months, a stillborn child was born. Another two months passed. Gudiya still did not get up from her bed. And slowly, her life-blood seeped out drip by drip, and Gudiya died.

The doctors said she did not have any major illness, yet she died, vomiting blood, inwardly and outwardly. She died little by little every day and then one day she welcomed death with open arms.

That little boy in the gaping hole, or the young man waiting for the gallows for the heinous rape whose daily routine inside the jail was described to stoke our lust for novelty, their very existence caught between life and death milked shamelessly for commercial gain, we at least did not allow them to die. But Gudiya? We, all of us, killed that young girl. Our voyeurism pierced her body like daggers, the rapier of our righteous attitudes cut her open and then dragged her to the deep hole of death and pushed her in. But in the process, she left behind a heavy load of guilt on our shoulders which, till her death, we did not even feel.

That burden has been getting heavier day by day though we try to ignore it by hiding behind the shadow of shame and guilt. We bend forward unable to bear the weight of the load. We have become like slaves to that all-pervading eye which lords over our vulgar, curious, thrill-seeking beings with its money and unlimited hold.

We could not bear the heat and heaviness of the humidity in the room and went up to the terrace to get some relief. But even there, hot air slapped our bodies as if the terrace was breathing it out and it even reached the soles of our feet.

In the twilight, beyond the landscape of thousands of lights, we saw a tall tower. A tower of light rising vertically to the sky. Looking at the ultra-modern futuristic architecture honed by an MNC, Abinash said, 'I don't know where I read about it, or maybe someone told me, or maybe I saw a sketch – my memory is deteriorating. It was perhaps in the Middle Ages or later. The place was somewhere in Europe – never mind, forget these unnecessary details. What's interesting is that the tower was constructed with a special plan. It was ensconced in the middle of a circle rising up to the sky defiantly. Encircling it was a row of prison cells. In them were kept the country's most feared criminals -- revolutionaries, enemies of the nation, dacoits, murderers. However, whether they were actually criminals, the pages of history have not revealed clearly, but it was sure that the authoritarian rulers regarded them as *jongis* (terrorists), and condemned them to prison till their death.

Extreme care was taken to build the prison in such a way that the inmates could be kept under surveillance all the time. Standing at the top of the tower, the leader and the guards often observed the prisoners, their eyes even reaching into the interior. Inside, the prisoners had no privacy. They stood naked before the probing eyes. Most importantly, the cells were built with ceilings so low that the inmates could never see the top of the tower. Just imagine that somebody is observing you with beady eyes all the time, your every move as you sleep, eat, your loneliness and anger, even when you defecate, urinate, masturbate. You perhaps know about it but can't do anything about it. You are helpless. You can't see him, so you can't even challenge him defiantly with fire in your eyes because he is invisible to you. At first, you burst out in anger and frustration but slowly you accept the futility of it all and accept the situation. Eventually, you become something like a lifeless object, without feelings, without an urge to even protest. How cruel it is – this process of slowly dehumanising someone. In fact, that tower was the symbol of this process by a state's autocratic power with a lust for unbridled control over others.

Standing still at the cusp of evening and night, we listened to Abinash's soliloquy and slowly in our mind an image of the unusual tower rose. Suddenly we felt that we too were prisoners in a circular complex, all of us. And from the peak of the tower in the middle an all-seeing phantom eye was observing us. It was playing a funny game with us. It opened its palm and on it we stood still without moving, like a helpless grasshopper. The eye looked up and down playfully, it tickled us sometimes, then as playfully wrenched a leg off from the body. It rode on strong wings to fly over the earth below. Look, it's chasing us now, wanting to see everything about us – the crevices of the body are stripped bare. The eye tries to hypnotise us, to reign over our decency and conscience in order to become the emperor of the kingdom peopled by millions of itchy-skin-scratchers.

There Will Be A Bridge

Juri Borah Borgohain

They all got up together – Moniram Dutta, Arif Siddiqui, Nabaneet Goswami. They left behind half-filled glasses, a plate of fried mutton kebabs. The smell of raw sliced onion hung in the air. Pulin Das was too drunk to move. His face was dotted with drops of perspiration. He brought out his handkerchief to wipe it off, but it was futile. Sweat trickled down his cheeks. The smooth sound of Nabaneet's new car disappeared into the distance. The ear-splitting sound of Moniram Dutta's Bullet motorbike also faded. Arif Siddiqui had perhaps walked to the venue.

Pulin Das switched on the TV again. One third of the wall was occupied by the huge LED TV screen. It was

---

Original Title: Eyat ekhon dolong hobo

now displaying Breaking News. The same announcement, again and again, by an excited announcer: 'There will be a bridge to the island.' The programme focused on the government's efforts, the joy of the people on the island, live telecast of a procession, and comments by some well-known leaders. A few faces barged in from behind in a vain attempt to be caught by the camera. It was accompanied by live shots of people dancing to the beat of the *dhol* and *khol* in celebration, and Bihu songs. Devotional Kirtan songs in praise of Lord Krishna were sung too. A couple of women ululated enthusiastically while facing the camera. Pulin Das sat up with a start. So many faces – some known, some unknown. The demand for the bridge had been pending for a long time. Many letters had been sent to the administration. Now at last, the government seemed to have heeded the public's demand. Within two to three years the bridge would come up as a symbol of development. The bridge could even be connected to the highway. Hence, there were many arguments in favour of the bridge.

Pulin Das had been running his business on this river island for a long time. He had inherited empty coffers but also a lot of cunning business sense. With his devious ways he had built up a clandestine empire. The island did not have a single wine shop. He took advantage of that to expand his business. All the high officials on the island were known to him, they were at his *adda* every evening. The local MLA, medium or small sycophantic leaders, contractors, student leaders – all were either his friends or known to him personally. Police officer Nabaneet Goswami, Arif Siddiqui of the Brahmaputra Board, Irrigation Department officer Moniram Dutta shared his wine and meat snacks. Like today, when they had congregated in the safe haven of his well-furnished air-conditioned room. Nobody disturbed them. The *adda* was at its zenith, and suddenly this news spoiled it all. They did not say anything but the mood was gone.

Pulin Das felt a bitter taste in his mouth. Siddiqui suddenly remembered about some chores he had to finish. Moniram Dutta suddenly remembered that he was supposed to do some grocery shopping in the bazaar. Nabaneet Goswami got a phone call from his boss. Now the huge silent room reverberated with the sound of the 700-watt Dolby stereo that seemed to be attacking him relentlessly. Sitting alone in the room, Pulin Das watched the Breaking News clip on the TV screen.

Pulin Das's sole aim in life was to make money. He worried that if the bridge came up within the next two years, the base of his empire would be eroded. After all, he had gained because there was no bridge. His illicit business had flourished like an Akashilata creeper. There was no problem with the excise department because it was all dealt with under the table. The large number of customers ensured his escalating profits. Though started with little investment, it had now grown exponentially. Once the bridge came up, his business would suffer. His power would erode too. Who knows but when the bridge becomes operational, it could start a regime of permits, excise duty, etc. Would some of his rivals take advantage of it? Though his business was no secret, once it was exposed, the flow of money would stop. He had spent years building up his position in society. His closeness to the important officers on the island helped elevate his stature among the people. The rustle of notes ensured luxury and easy access to whatever he wanted. His wife and children looked up to him. But most of all, he had arrived. It was something that he had craved for, coming from a position where he had nothing. He was extremely conscious of this good fortune. If he lost his source of wealth he would have to go back to his life of poverty and want, a past he hated – a man without a roof over his head, hungry all the time, and looked down upon by society.

Ah, how Pulin Das hated poverty!

He perspired more and wiped his face with the handkerchief. His eyes remained riveted on the TV screen.

(2)

Pranjal took the call from the MLA and then looked around the room.

'The bridge will be built, after all. The TV news says so. I hear that it's going live. I have been told by Sir to give bytes for the TV programme.'

His cronies from the *sanstha* threw away their playing cards and jumped up in joy.

'Wow, Pranjal-da! This MLA is different, we must say. He was elected only a few months ago.'

'What are you are talking about? You think it's due to the MLA? Who created a hullabaloo demanding the bridge? I! Do you see what I have achieved?'

Pranjal thumped his chest with the arrogance of a leader.

'You guys go. We will have a party tonight. Arrange it. I'll join you after meeting the TV reporter.'

'Pranjal-da, what about the bottle...?'

'Go tell Pulin-da, mention my name.'

The boys left together on their motorbikes in a cacophony of noise. There were some sounds of elated whistling and then everything became silent. Pranjal lighted a cigarette. So the bridge would be built. They would take two years to complete it. On the surface, he had led a campaign to build it but actually, he had opposed it. He had secretly signed the papers of the opposing party. He had himself gone to meet the governor to give that paper. They said that the bridge would destroy the historical significance of the island and its cultural heritage would suffer. As a student leader, he received a handsome 'cut' from all involved – from the MLA's fund for building the spur on the riverbank, from Pulin Das, Binod Hazarika who owned the ferry service, and community leader Deben Payeng. The commission from the Brahmaputra Board and the Irrigation Department were separate. If he was not given the money, he threatened to join the campaign for the bridge. After a few days of processions, campaigns and hunger strike, the funds arrived, like rain in the monsoon season. The agitation stopped after that. There was no more campaigning for the bridge, no procession. Pranjal Nath's pockets had been filled and he planned to go for a vacation in the hills of Shillong and Cherrapunji. To make it more enjoyable one or two young women would accompany him. Now all this will disappear after two years. Nor will there be the heady intoxication of being a leader; the MLA who forked out a lakh of rupees instantly on demand for his 'right hand man' Pranjal, might not care to do so any more. He considered his achievements – his two tankers to carry oil in Digboi, the oil depot in Teok, the three-storeyed house coming up in Jorhat. Few knew about his eventual plans to move away from the island. All this was due to his position as a leader on the island. The lure of being a leader was hard to ignore. Besides, he had a secret dream which nobody knew about. He wanted to hijack the MLA's agenda and somehow manage a ticket from the party before the next election.

Thus his position in the forefront would be assured. He was always in demand, whether at community meetings, weddings, or even to intermediate in political conflicts between two parties. He had learnt how to be popular with people through social work. But now all this, the semblance of being busy, the pride of being in demand everywhere, promise of a golden future, would be gone though he might not lack money.

Then there was the matter of Nandita. She had rejected him till now. He planned to make a last attempt to win her as his wife. He would try to lure her with his money and position. After all, he was getting on in years and should settle down. Now Nandita will win and he will be defeated. Once the bridge was built, he would lose his position too. He would become a nonentity. Pranjal broke out in a sweat at the thought. He searched for a handkerchief in his pocket. He kicked at the chair in anger. It crashed onto the floor. The sound filled the silent room.

(3)

Binod Hazarika was hosting a party for the Press. For the past couple of days, the matter of impending fare increase on the ferry was making news. He had to do something about it. He had to keep his record clean. Otherwise, he would not be able to take part in the auction of the ghat next time. He could see that quite a few claimants had emerged hoping to take control of the ghats.

Most of the reporters were there. There were three ghats and six ferries were supposed to operate from there. Salary for the lessee and payment for the temporary labourers had to be managed. From the reporters to the police, the MLA and the water department – all had to be bribed, kept happy. So, the fare had to be hiked. He had to explain all this and see to it that the news of the fare hike was smothered. That was the reason for this elaborate arrangement. The well-appointed air-conditioned guesthouse was ready to welcome the reporters. Drinks and various dishes with meat were also ready. Some of them did not take alcoholic drinks. For them Pepsi and Coca-Cola had been arranged. Everybody in the family was busy too. After a long time, his wife had come to the island. She was dressed tastefully and moved around among the guests. She was slim and all eyes were on her firm but full breasts. Hazarika did not like it when his wife talked with the young men, and the *aanchal* of her saree slipped more often. Anyway, he let it pass. As long as the job was done, he was happy. He imagined himself later in the night in her arms and felt quite excited about the prospect.

Suddenly the news flashed on the TV screen and the whole atmosphere changed instantly. The reporters jumped up excitedly. The mobile phones came alive with calls. A few took leave of Mrs Hazarika. The expensive bottle of alcohol that Pulin Das had sent, the smoked pork, the fried chicken, the cashew nuts, were all abandoned.

Hazarika felt his head reeling. For the last 20 years, he had ruled the ghats with his ferry business. The two houses in Guwahati, three plots of land in Jorhat town were all thanks to it. His wife, his children stayed in different houses. The connection to the island was strictly business oriented. All these years, he had enjoyed portions of fish and meat that passed through the ghat, besides milk, petrol, and good alcohol. Because he was the boss of the ghat, he also enjoyed the company of a couple of Mising tribe girls. He was the king of the island. This time he had sought a ticket to stand for the election but failed. He knew that ultimately, he would get what he wanted.

But now a bridge in two years... only two years! He mumbled to himself.

As his wife passed by, her *aanchal* slipped from her breasts. Was it deliberate? She seemed to look at him pityingly. Hazarika felt crushed.

(4)

A few months earlier.

'Please sign, Prabhu Iswar!' Though she addressed the Sattradhikar with due respect as befitting his position as head of the *sattra,* the Vaishnavite ashram, her voice had a commanding note. There was no sign of servitude of in it. He looked at her. She was not sitting with her head bowed as did other disciples in his monastery. She stood confidently, demanding his attention unapologetically.

The Sattradhikar did not reply for some time. Her father was a well-wisher of this sattra. He had donated land to build dormitories for the students at the ashram. They had been *bhakts* of the *sattra* for many generations. He was polite and had approached the Sattradhikar for advice on various occasions. He even confided in him about household affairs and took a decision only after seeking his counsel. But look at his daughter, she was so arrogant! Why was she like this? She was bright, admittedly, but she was too argumentative. Was it because she had studied somewhere else, far away from home and had the courage to defy him and the traditions of the *sattra*? She spoke to him without bowing. Nor did she kneel before him. It was something unheard of in the ancient *sattra*. He felt distracted, tense and irritated. But he could not show it and wore an artificial, calm smile. It was a matter of habit with him.

The petition was spread out in front of him – a long one. Quite a few well-known personalities had signed it. Among them were a couple of heads of other *sattras*.

However, they were not considered as significant. He and a few others were the ones who were considered important by the community. His signature was valuable.

Nandita had been leading the campaign for the bridge for a long time. She had written in the media about the problem, and the importance of the bridge for the island's people. Slowly, she was becoming a well-known figure on the island. This also made the Sattradhikar a little jealous. He was afraid. He was afraid that he would lose his position in the local society. This made him restless. He had built his image over a long period of time. He had a serene smile, his forehead was lined with sandalwood paste, and he was dressed in white silk. People respected him. He had money, he enjoyed luxury. From business contactors to political leaders, all approached him for favour. He was proud of it. He wanted to cling to these privileges till death.

Now this girl was here with this appeal. She sought his signature. The government had accepted the request in principle. Now what was needed was cooperation from the people and organisations on the island. She had come earlier too. Quite a few Sattradhikars, a few journalists and a few contractors declined to sign the petition. He was one of them. Now it seemed the bridge was going to be built after all. He had watched the discussions on TV and felt the winds were blowing in its favour. He had to take advantage of the time. Perhaps a few reporters would come, also TV correspondents. They would ask for his reaction to the impending announcement. He must put up a façade of happiness at the prospect. It was a welcome move; he must applaud it.

Actually, whether there was a bridge or not, it would not affect him. He had his own personal ferry and could go anywhere at any time he wished. He did not have a family to worry about. The river had offered him a certain position in public. After two years, if the bridge came up, would his prestige remain? With it, would enter the modern age. It would blow away the servitude and devotion that the *sattras* had commanded from Vaishnav apprentices for centuries. They would defy the customs that had continued in the name of *dharma*. He would lose his unquestioned authority. His *sattra* had survived on the beliefs and dependence of the common people. His popularity had increased by leaps and bounds in the past few years. He was at the forefront at meetings and gatherings. He was apprehensive that he would lose all this, if the bridge came up.

Frustrated, worried, he pulled the paper with the appeal towards him. His eyes ran over the signatories quickly. The girl pulled the cap off the pen. He signed the paper.

'Thank you!'

She gathered the paper and without touching his feet, as was wont, left and walked down the steps from the *sara-ghar* where he met visitors. Labourers were putting tiles on the stairs. Now as she hurried down she stumbled a bit and her toe dislodged a piece of the tile. '*Khat.*' The rude sound broke the silence of the place. A few *bhakts* who sat hunched on their knees looked on, astonished.

The Sattradhikar wiped the perspiration from his face with the end of the white *seleng (*shawl) on his shoulder. He saw two newspaper reporters in the distance coming towards the *sattra*. He tried hard to bring out his ever-familiar serene smile to greet them.

(5)

Pulin Das called Pranjal Nath. He did not pick up the phone.

Pranjal Nath called Binod Hazarika. The phone was busy.

Binod Hazarika was on the phone with Deben Payeng. Payeng was trying to connect with the MLA on the phone.

The MLA was trying to reach the Sattradhikar. At that time, the Sattradhikar was busy in front of the TV camera. Smiling serenely, he was airing his thoughts on the need for a bridge. His phone was in silent mode.

(6)

By the time Nandita got onto the ferry, it was full. It was so crowded with bikes, cars, baskets of the raw fish, huge jugs of milk, bunches of bananas in hessian bags, a few goats tied together with rope, that there was hardly any room to stand. She knew many of the people, some she did not. She saw Girish-da from their village. He looked distressed. He seemed restless and his eyes had a lost look. She was about to address him when he himself came forward and said: 'Your 'bou' is not well. The doctor had asked me to take her to Jorhat yesterday. But I couldn't. The ghat timings were over. She is suffering a lot. We'll take an hour and a half to reach the other bank, right?'

Girish-da wiped his face worriedly.

'The pain actually began the day before yesterday. Today she seems half-dead.'

Nandita craned her neck. From a gap in the crowd, she saw Girish-da's wife lying on the narrow bench. Her pregnant stomach was distended and she was obviously in pain.

'Couldn't you get the ambulance ferry?' she asked.

'It's been lying defunct for quite some time now,' Girish said.

Suddenly his wife screamed. Girish ran to her. Nandita tried to reach her through the crowd. The people were agitated too but made way for her. She found Girish's mother massaging coconut oil on the woman's head and fanning her. The pregnant woman was holding onto the wooden bench tightly. Nandita could see that she was in extreme pain. Her skin was pale and she looked very weak. She was moaning faintly. It was a pitiful sight.

Ghot, ghot, ghot, ghot...

The ferry was on its way. But the people were not talking today like on other days. They were all anxious, worried. The pathetic moans of Girish's wife invaded their thoughts.

'O *Bouti* I'm dying,' the heart-rending cry caught at Nandita's heartstrings. She saw that from between her legs a reddish stream like murky water was flowing out. Her scream surpassed the *ghot-ghot* sound of the ferry's engine.

'Hey, bring a *sador* to screen the woman. She's having the baby,' Girish-da's mother shouted.

She pushed Nandita aside and snatched the *seleng* from the shoulder of a passenger. He was a *bhakt* of a *sattra*. So, behind the clean white cloth screen, her *mekhela* wet with blood, the woman gave birth to a baby.

But Nandita was worried. She could see that the blood was streaming down continuously from between the legs of the woman she called 'bou'. Girish-da's mother wanted to wrap the baby in the *seleng* but stopped. Her daughter-in-law was still shaking with pain. Now, the woman was not moaning but was taking long gasping breaths. The only sounds were the *ghot-ghot* sound of the ferry and the bleating of the goats. A few passengers tried to peek at the woman.

Nandita closed her eyes. She didn't know that a human body could hold so much blood. Suddenly she observed that her *bou* was not moving at all; she was lying very still. After a few minutes, she could see that she was not breathing. She looked at the Girish-da's mother.

'Mother and child, both gone,' she uttered the words as if they were coming from the deepest recesses of her heart. She folded the *seleng*. The raw smell of blood from the uterus of Girish-da's wife filled the ferry. The soft body of the baby was covered with blood. Next to him was the still body of his mother. It was something Nandita had never seen before, never experienced. The suddenness of it all made her dumb with shock. How cruel, how heart-rending the whole scene was!

She did not dare find out what Girish-da was doing. The wails of his mother rose above the irritating mechanical sound of the ferry.

With 150 passengers, Nandita too was waiting to reach the other bank.

She remembered how a few days ago, a sudden storm had forced the ferry to stop midway. It was quite dark. Mothers with little kids were crying in despair. The hungry kids were crying too. Taking advantage of the darkness, somebody had tried to molest a pretty Mising girl. How shameful was that moment. She had roundly abused him. Then she cried. Another ferry arrived at midnight to rescue the people.

One day, her old friend had jumped into the Brahmaputra in front of her. She was devastated that her husband was having an affair with another woman. She had instantly disappeared in the whirlpool in the river. Her mother howled inconsolably. People sat around her helplessly for two hours.

And of course there was Monikankona Gam. That girl, who sang beautifully, had breathed her last on the ferry. People on that the ferry had cried at the demise of the girl who had brought fame to the island with her singing prowess. The ferry had returned to the ghat after travelling halfway down the river.

Kalpajyoti had refused to marry Nandita blaming the inconvenience of the location of her house.

'My parents don't want to bring a daughter-in-law from across the river,' he had said as an excuse.

It was an insult to Nandita who had just returned from Delhi after finishing her studies. Her romance with Kalpajyoti had died unexpectedly.

Today she had witnessed another death.

She came out of the shade avoiding the now silent passengers. She saw that the river bank was coming into view. She wondered if she should look at the still body of the woman she called bou. She did not have the courage to do so.

The ferry was near the ghat now. For Girish-da it did

not have any meaning now.

Nandita could hear the Girish-da's mother still wailing. Groups of people were crowding the bank, waiting to cross the river on this ferry to reach the island.

The strain of the journey, the uncertainty, sick patients, cows and goats travelling with the passengers, the overwhelming smell of raw fish, fear of the overloaded ferry sinking, storm and rain bringing additional danger, fear of hitting the sandbank – all this will perhaps become history once the bridge was built.

Nandita had collected lots of signatures. Today, there was no group opposing the bridge. She would deliver the petition to the deputy commissioner of upper Assam. She would tell him that unlike what he and some administrators thought, people on the island did not have any objection to the bridge. Look, everybody has signed – from student leader Pranjal Nath to the Sattradhikar Harikanta Goswami.

Now please start the work.

The people were waiting. And hoping. Nandita was determined play a part in giving shape to the dream.

She knew it would take time. Yet...

Before she alighted from the ferry, Nandita looked back. Girish-da's mother was holding the dead baby close to her chest. Girish-da was covering his dead wife's body with a *seleng* with great care.

The Trick

Monikuntala Bhattacharjya

'How far is Anu's house from here?'

'Why are you asking me? Don't you know that I can see only with one eye?'

The Crow said, twisting around to answer her. To tell the truth, she did not want to tell the girl that she knew where Anu's house was. Renu was unaware of that. She was a rather simple girl but she was not stupid. She was known as a part of *Padartha* (substance). And now she was asking about Anu, which literally means the basic indivisible atom of a substance. She knew that both the girls were planning strategies to entice Padartha, the boy. Anu was the cleverer of the two. She dressed in the latest fashion and made it a point to go for a walk past

---

Original Title: Koushal

Padartha's house in the afternoon. Renu was the kind of girl who would stand at the gate of her house to get a glimpse of Padartha on his way to college, more like the lovelorn girls of old. On the other hand, the Crow was a nonentity who owned a small stall. She observed all these proceedings but pretended not to notice. She sold *paan* – areca nut wrapped in betel leaf, biscuits, bindis, soap, toffee, etc. in her nondescript stall. Renu's contemporaries did not know her real name. While addressing her, they called her *mahi* (aunt), but behind her back they referred to her as The Crow. She would talk nineteen to the dozen in her off-key voice. One of her eyes was completely white. The creator did not bother to put even a black spot there. Or perhaps He did not have enough time. She managed with one eye but if she had to look at something she had to move her neck side-to-side, like a crow, for a better view. This earned her the sobriquet The Crow.

The Crow found Padartha very simple. He was handsome, well-bred and a gentleman to the core. Yet, he was known as Padartha, a thing or a substance, among his friends. Wherever he was, a circle of friends gathered around him. He did not speak much but whatever he said was so witty that people could not help laughing. His rather sombre mien did not reveal the kind of thoughts he carried in his head. A friend commented one day, 'You are really a thing, an item, I must say.'

'Not item or thing, say *padartha,* it gives a smart ring to the word.' From that day he became known as Padartha.

The Crow did not know all this. When he came to buy cigarettes, she called him Bhaiti (younger brother). Sometimes he drove down in his father's car and stopped in front of her shop, which lent it an extra dignity. At this time, her cawing would increase in volume. Perhaps to avoid talking to her, he would take out his mobile phone from his pocket, search for something on the screen and speak to someone. The Crow did not pay much attention to it. But one day she did. He pushed at some numbers and then spoke, 'Hello! This is Padartha...'

The Crow was going to put some lime paste on the betel leaf but stopped abruptly. Did she hear right? She had never come across such an odd name.

The boy was still talking. She observed him from behind. Ah, his manners, his demeanour were very much like a *zamindar's* (landlord's) son.

She sighed. Perhaps his parents had given him this name for some personal reason. After all, big people were different from people like her.

She sighed again and continued with her work. She chewed a paan and stared at the road in front, thinking of the names she had given to her children.

She, however, continued to call him Bhaiti. She tried to say Padartha, but felt shy and tongue-tied. Padartha.

What kind of a name was that? Did she hear correctly? But her doubts were cleared when a friend of his joined him and addressed him as Padartha.

After she closed the shop, she went to the kitchen. She was trying to light the fire with the still damp firewood when all of a sudden, a kick landed on her back. This kind of attack was a sign of cowardice. She stood up with the *sunga.* She thought for a moment, why not hit him back with this weapon? But she refrained. She could, but she did not. She threw the bamboo pipe at the wall and like a small girl, whimpered, threw up her hands and took to her bed.

Her husband was a cook in a restaurant. He could have had his food there but instead he always brought along his share of fish or meat to have with his children. Sometimes on the way home, when he stopped by a den to have a drink with his cronies, his packet became a little lighter. That would instigate a physical attack on his wife. But crows are sly too. If she could bear a little bit of this torture, the purpose was served. He would struggle to light the raw firewood stove to start cooking dinner himself. Meanwhile, she could lie down and rest after a whole day of labour. He would grumble all the time while he cooked, 'This is how you maintain the house? You can't even cook a meal. Useless!'

But she did not care. She was happy to close her eyes, with the pillow hugged to her chest.

The day she came to know that there was a person called Padartha, she started pondering on the choice adjectives her husband showered on her every night when he came home. She now started treating it in a different way. When he called her *apadartha*, meaning useless, she in fact liked it, the smell of Sewali flower filled her heart, simply because *apadartha* rhymed with *padartha*. How could she regard it as abuse? How she loved the personality of the boy! How well-mannered he was and sophisticated too! If a man like him could be nicknamed Padartha, what was wrong if a drunken man called her *apadartha*? She didn't mind.

Meanwhile she tried to imitate Padartha's polite manners.

On a day like this, Renu came to her shop.

'Do you have laundry soap, Mahi?' she asked.

'What?'

'Soap to wash clothes.'

'Yes, I have but I was about to go to the *teeniali* junction. There's not a single cigarette in my shop now.'

'Are there people around here who smoke? I find that most of them are old people and are used to chewing ground areca nut with betel leaf.'

'Oh, listen to you! Wait, let me give you the soap in the meantime. Of course, there are people who like cigarettes.'

She hurriedly gave Renu a slab of rough washing

soap. But just as she extended her hand to take the money from her, she fell into a tizzy, exclaiming, 'Here he comes! What do I do now? I don't have a single pack of cigarettes in the shop.'

Renu turned her head towards the road to check who had come to make the woman so nervous. Instantly, her face changed colour. He was from the well-off family that had recently shifted into the rented house next to the Shiva temple. Her heart thumped like the beat of the *bhor-taal* cymbal. She often stood near the gate of her house to get a glimpse of this boy and now he was striding towards the shop.

Her body trembled but she tried to act normal and asked casually, 'Who is he, Mahi?'

'Why, can't you see? Padartha!'

'Padartha? What are you saying?'

Renu found it very strange. How could that be a name?

But by now he was in front of the shop. He was speaking to someone on the mobile phone. Without stopping, he stretched his hand out to The Crow. By now, Renu was almost hidden behind the jars in the shop. She felt inadequate.

'Sorry, Bhaiti, today I don't have any,' The Crow said.

'Hello, please hold on for a minute. What did you say? You don't have cigarettes today?'

The Crow moved her pale eye to a corner and said

politely, 'No. I was just going to the junction to get some when she came to get this *dhela* soap and I couldn't go. Please don't mind.'

'That's all right,' he said.

He returned to his cell phone and looked at Renu. Her brows were creased unhappily. Why did The Crow have to mention the rough cheap soap in front of him? She felt embarrassed. What would he think? That she was poor or stingy. At least, she could have mentioned something more appropriate.

But she admitted to herself that there were no commodities in The Crow's shop one could call glamorous and forgave her. She straightened herself when she found that Padartha was looking at her. Was she looking all right? She had combed her hair casually before leaving house; was it looking okay? She had shampooed her hair the day before yesterday. Was it shining enough today? Thank God, she had trimmed her eyebrows with a blade while she was at the study table this morning.

She turned to the things displayed in The Crow's shop. Oh God, she had come dressed in the churidar kameez set she had worn at home. The colour was slightly faded. The fitting was good though. Was she looking all right?

'Do you want anything else?' The Crow asked her politely.

Renu was caught off guard. An intelligent person

would catch the hint immediately. She understood that she should leave now and she did.

That Renu, whose name meant pollen of a flower, returned home not as *renu* but as a particle of *padartha*.

Back home she realised that the feeling she had nursed for the young man had now turned into something more serious. Padartha, ah, Padartha! I have become a part of you, can't you feel it? I love you! I think of you all the time. I hug you close to my breast. Can't you feel my presence in the ether around you? I can't live without you, I love you deeply, Padartha-da.

Though Padartha enjoyed his life as a carefree young man, he was a man after all. He also had a malleable heart. At this age the heart wants to run fast, like stitches on a sewing machine... *khat, khat...khat.*

He pulled up the collar of his T-shirt. These girls posed problems at times, complaining: 'Don't look there, don't go there.'

'I called you but you ignored me.'

'You don't love me these days.'

'I'd write letters, I don't have a mobile like you.'

And then requesting, 'I don't want earrings, please present me with a mobile. I can then talk to you the whole night.'

Whoa, what trouble! He had somehow managed to buy one for himself but had to beg his mother to pay the bill and now the girlfriend wanted him to buy her a mobile phone! No, it was better to remain like this, with no interest in girls.

How did The Crow guess all these thoughts going on in his head? With her usual habit of observing people, she looked at him closely. He seemed to blow away his worries with the smoke rings he blew into the air.

Good, good, he was keeping himself away from girls. He should pass from the college with good marks and go elsewhere to study and become a doctor or lawyer, she thought to herself. The girls would always try to set a trap but does it mean you need to walk into it blindly? No, none of these girls here deserves you. You smoke as much as you want. And ponder on anything you want, but don't allow yourself to be cornered. Let God help you to escape from this situation.

But one day she observed that he forgot to smoke and became a little restless as he saw Anu passing by with a friend. After that, she kept an eye on Anu with her one eye.

That day Padartha was enjoying an *adda* with his friends and smoking when Anu came to her shop accompanied with a little boy.

One of Padartha's friends asked the boy, 'What's your name, Bhaiti?'

'Ankur. He is my uncle's son,' Anu answered instead. The Crow was not happy at her forwardness. But Padartha, though pretending not to, was looking at her.

'What are you looking for?' The Crow asked. She

wanted to get rid of the girl as soon as possible.

'I don't want anything. I just came like that.'

'Came like that?'

It was as if The Crow's nest had been set on fire but she kept her cool and maintained her newly acquired politeness and said, 'That's fine. I thought you had come to buy something. Please don't mind.'

'No, no, why should I mind? I just came for a walk. I was getting bored of sitting at the study table all day.'

'Yes, you are right. There's a limit to how much you can study in a day. You are welcome to come any day, we can talk. But today I won't keep you waiting. You can see the crowd here. If another customer comes there won't be room to even stand. This little boy is your brother, is it? What's your name? Oh, Ankur is it? Wait, I'll give you a lozenge. You can share with your sister.'

The little boy nodded happily.

The Crow gave him two sweets and put the lid back on the bottle. She said, 'Have it, okay? Now you go, go for a walk with your sister.'

What could Anu do now? She left, her ponytail bouncing at every step. On the way back, she smiled shyly at Padartha. He also seemed to respond with a smile though he was also talking to his friends.

The Crow's thoughts now spread like the branches of a tree. Renu, Anu, Anu, Renu, which one of them would get Padartha's attention? After all, as they say, even an elephant slips sometimes.

Which of them would suit his personality? Renu had a soft look but her manners and looks were slightly old-fashioned. Anu was very fair and stylish but too thin.

She sighed deeply and pushed the firewood sticks into the stove. You could not trust these men. Once her husband made no bones about the fact that she was too thin and he did not enjoy holding her. She had been crestfallen. If she could not put on weight, what could she do? Now she had a rounder figure, more to his liking. But did he compliment her? Never! Men! Look at yourselves! If we women judge you on the scale of good looks, good behaviour or personality, you won't even make it to the lowest rung.

True, you can't guess whom a man likes. Even your shadow won't know who he finds attractive. These days thin girls seemed to be in fashion.

She sighed again and moved the ladle in the wok. If he kicked her today, she decided, she would strike him with the ladle. The wood was drier today, she could cook easily. Though he was proud of it, what was his skill as a cook anyway, she sneered inwardly, adding all that red chilli powder to the curry. Did he think their kitchen was his eatery serving customers who slurped on the hot curry?

'Ma, I am very sleepy. Please give me dinner.'

One of her kids whined but she screamed at him. In a

second, her veneer of good manners disappeared.

'What do you think? You ask for food and you'll get it instantly? If you are sleepy, go to the bed. I am only human, how much can I do? Don't go on whimpering, I'll beat you senseless. Haven't you seen my temper?'

As soon as she finished, from outside came the familiar shout

'Oi, who are you going to beat senseless? Useless, *apadartha*! Wait, you'll get it now.'

There was the sound of a stick being broken off from the bamboo fence.

The ladle in The Crow's hand trembled. Quickly she went to hide in a corner behind the door. But her effort was useless as he entered the room.

The next day she went to open the shop even as her shins bore the welt marks of the bamboo stick. She yawned from time to time. In her agitation she could not sleep at night. Only now she had got some respite. Ah, what a lovely breeze! She closed her eyes in bliss.

'Mahi, can I get some soda bicarb?'

It was Renu.

'Oh, this is our Renu! I was a bit sleepy. Now tell me, what's the news? How was your Matric exam?'

'It was so-so.'

'No, no, don't say that. You look very bright. When will the results come out?'

'Around March, I think.'

'Don't worry, it'll be all right. Is it already time now to prepare for the Test for the next class X exam?'

'No there's time. Why, is there anyone you know who needs help?'

'Why, there's Anu.'

'Who is this Anu?'

'The girl who dresses up all the time.'

'Okay.'

'That day she came here and talked about the pressure of studies. They were also here, Padartha and gang.'

Renu felt a tightening in her chest. But she was a girl more in control and like in the olden days, she could hide it. She asked casually, 'Did she come to buy something?'

'No, nothing. She came with her uncle's son. Actually, I thought that she had come, like you, to buy something. But she said that she was tired of studying the whole day and so came to have a chat with me. I was surprised, of course. Still, I gave the boy a few lozenges and told him, why didn't he go to for a walk? There were so many customers around and there was no space to even stand. So she had to leave. But I saw how she gave a special look to Padartha. He has quite sober manners. But nowadays the boys seem to like sprightly girls without much substance, what can I say.'

The next day, Renu came again. She looked quite grave.

'Mahi, how are you?'

'Pulling along somehow.'

'Do you have tobacco leaf, the kind my grandmother takes?'

'Yes, I have, wait. And what's the news?'

'Well, I wanted to ask how far Anu's house from here is.'

A few days later, Anu came to the shop.

'How are you, Mahi?'

'I am pulling along somehow. What about you?'

'I am fine. But look at the gloomy weather!'

'Yes, you are right. But I don't think you need anything, you've come to meet me, right?'

She smiled shyly. The Crow turned her neck sideways and mentioned, 'That day Renu had come. She was about to leave after the purchase but I said, wait a moment, let's have a chat. Oh, by the way he was also waiting here.'

'Who?'

'Wait, I forget his name. You know, the boy from the house near the Shiva temple, very handsome, the one who goes to the college... Damn, what's happened to my memory? Anyway he was here and the way they exchanged looks! But I caught them anyway. How can they hide from me? So she left hurriedly. But I must say, both of them match very well. Sorry, I can't remember his name.'

Anu, the indivisible atom in Padartha's substance seemed to break into smithereens. Still, she spoke nonchalantly.

'Manas Pratim.'

'What?'

The Crow got a shock. What was this girl saying?

'But his name is Padartha.'

'How can that be the name of a person? It could be a nickname given to nonentities who show an interest in girls like Renu. Okay, let me leave now.'

'Wait, wait!'

'What?'

'So Padartha is not his real name?'

'I told you so. Let me go now.'

'Hey, listen!'

'What?'

'Should I tell you or not?'

'Please tell me.'

'That day Renu asked me for your address. But why should I tell her?'

'Why? Why does she want to know? Are you talking about that common girl from the gloomy house near the bamboo grove? They even have a cowshed in the front yard.'

'Yes, yes, you are right.'

'But why does she want to know the location of my house?'

'Why, don't you know? Isn't the house where Padartha, I mean Manas or something, lives just one house away from yours? She wants to see him from up close, you see.'

'What? I'll tear her hair out!'

'No, no, don't speak like that.'

'Please tell her, she shouldn't try all these things with me.'

'I think she understood it after the way I snubbed her.'

'What rubbish! These men!'

'Yes, I agree. I considered him to be a nice boy but I see it's otherwise.'

'You are right, of course! What a bad choice! And a girl like Renu, of all things.'

'Look, he is coming this way! To blow away his father's money, of course!'

'I am leaving, Mahi!'

'Sure!'

Now The Crow sat down more comfortably. She felt relieved but sat with a gloomy face. He took the cigarette from her then noticing the woman's woebegone face, he asked, 'Are you feeling all right?'

'I am fine. But I was thinking of something else. You, all people.'

'What happened?'

'Just now the one who has left?'

'Hmm?'

'That day another girl had come, remember?'

'Yes, but what's the problem?'

'Oh, I feel bad to reveal what they think.'

'Please tell me.'

'How can I say this?'

'Why not?'

'You must promise it won't get out.'

'Trust me, you can tell me.'

'They come to meet you. Both of them come here to see you and they harass me, asking about you.'

'What rubbish! Don't pay any attention to the stupid girls.'

'You don't do either.'

'What do you think? I don't have time to think about these things. You have seen me, haven't you, all these days? I don't even wait here for long.'

'Yes, you are right.'

The Crow nodded her head again and again, agreeing with him.

At night, sitting near the stove, even after slapping the whimpering child, she wondered, 'Why was Renu asking the direction to Anu's house?'

That bothered her. So next time Renu came to the shop she asked point blank.

Renu smiled shyly and said, 'I am sitting around idle till the exam results come out. I have started giving private tuition to the next batch of students appearing for the Matric exam. I wondered if Anu would be interested. I already have two students, but can take two more or so. So, I thought I would ask her.'

'Okay.'

The Crow sits nonchalantly, waiting for a better life. The country, the future generation, who cares about them?

In her beak she holds a piece of meat. Of aspiration. She is a crow of this age, not of the Aesop's Fables where the fox had tricked the crow to sing with flattery and got his prize. She is today's crow, capable of getting rid of the fox with her own tricks.

The Areca Nut Tree

Manika Devee

The man was eager. He made overtures to his wife. It was tacit. A man does not waste time with words. The wife should instinctively understand that her husband wants to have sex with her. And this bed where they retired for the night was meant for it, wasn't it? There was no excuse for not understanding this simple truth. The man was not ready to wait. His body burnt with desire.

He tossed and turned restlessly a couple of times. The wooden bed shook. How could any woman not respond to this invitation? Yet she lay like a piece of wood beside him.

Original Title: Kakini

Yes, like a piece of wood. She lay there as though she was dead. The pain was unbearable. She was unable to lie down on her back and so turned to one side of her body to get some relief. Her back bore witness to the severe beating she had received from her husband that day. The streaks of coagulated blood criss-crossed her back. The stick he used to restrain the cows almost broke in two when he beat her with it. She shivered at the memory. And after all this, what did he expect? That she would dance around him like a butterfly? She ground her teeth, livid with anger.

The man was also gnashing his teeth in anger. The rage that overcame him at midday spurted out again. Well, at that time she had taken too long to pour water into the glass from the pitcher, but now? Now there was no reason to be late in responding to him. Her body was full of promise, the lush figure was there to be taken. All he wanted was a little response from her. But she did not show any interest. Oh, how could one bear this show of defiance? What was he going to do? Beat her up again? Every strike would give some relief to his increasing impatience to devour her body. No, it was not possible now. His desire could not be tamed in any other way. He was not going to wait for her to come to him willingly. He was going to enjoy his right as a husband. He snatched away the *aanchal* covering her breasts.

You can take away a piece of cloth covering the

breasts easily, but can you whittle down the mountain of bitterness building inside her heart? She jumped down from the bed, opened the bamboo door and walked out onto the veranda without fear. Whom would she fear anyway? The granary at the corner, with legs like bamboo poles? The kitchen, looming like a monster, that exhaled fumes all day? Or the big room, on the opposite side, like a witch's lair where her mother-in-law and her two sisters-in-law slept? The house, full of sounds during the day, was now silent, each corner confined to its own lair as if wrapped under a comfortable quilt.

The courtyard was awash in silvery moonlight. But, perhaps because of her tears streaming down her cheeks like rain, she saw only a cloudy sky.

She was the only daughter in her family. Her *pita* (father) never called her anything but *Ai* (my little mother). Her older brother would wait to eat even a morsel of food till his *bhoni* (beloved sister) joined him. If her mother scolded her for any reason, they would rise to her defence. And this man, her husband, never once asked her, 'Did I hurt you too much? I don't know how it happened in my rage. Come, let me look at your back, take off your blouse.' But why should he look at her back? What was there to see anyway? God had given that portion of the body to women to receive beatings from men. Right! It was quite a neglected part of her body.

And what grave mistake had she committed to deserve

such punishment, to have her back covered with bruises? Admitted, he had returned from the field tired after a long day. He had asked for a glass of water. Through an opening in the reed wall of the kitchen, she had got a glimpse of his sunburnt face. But she was busy at that time. The wok was on the firewood stove and the oil in it was smoking as she prepared to season the *dal* (lentil curry). Though the house was full of people, there was no one around whom she could ask to watch over the wok. They were, however, all too ready to criticise her when they sat down to lunch. Too much salt, the curry had a burnt smell, the gourd was under-cooked, etc., etc. Like the various bowls arranged around their brass plates at lunchtime, their complaints were numerous and assorted.

She took off the hot pan from the wooden fire. Just when she poured the glass of water, he came at her. He caught hold of her thick hair and shouted, 'Can't you hear me? Should I wait the whole day for a glass of water? I have spent all day under the sun and here she is traipsing around like a peacock. *Saali, haramzadi* (obscenities)!'

Her long hair had loosened from the bun. But even the thick hair could not save her back.

His shouts broke the silence of the night, 'Showing off your temper, are you? I'll cut you in two, you'll see!'

Leaning against the bamboo pole supporting the veranda, she wept silently, like the first wife spurned by the king.